ESSENCE

A SECOND DOSE

DIANE STRINGAM TOLLEY

Lydia

Jackson W

Diane Stringam Tolley

ESSENCE

A SECOND DOSE

DIANE STRINGAM TOLLEY

Summary: Todd and his father, a famous scientist are
kidnapped and forced to continue their work in captivity
while they plot to escape.

ISBN-13: 978-1530949083
ISBN-10: 1530949084

Cover Photo by **Mariya Ermolaeva**
Cover design © 2016 by Diane Stringam Tolley
Edited by Caitlin Clark

Dedication

Essence: A Second Dose

is dedicated to all the animal
lovers of the world.

Wouldn't you just love to be one?

And to Ryan. My biggest fan.

Chapter One

"Todd!" Rich looked disgusted. "How could you miss a shot like that? You're shooting like a blind man!" Rich was sitting on the couch, both feet propped up on the coffee table. He waved a half-finished hot dog. "You do realize you're letting yourself be beaten by a woman!"

"Hah. Totally!" JoJo got to her feet.

"Please be kind!" I whimpered as I flopped down on the couch.

"You're going down, Iverson!"

She lifted her controller and took aim. "This time, it's all 100 pins!" She swung her arm and cleared the alley.

"You're very hard on my ego, Jo," I told her, getting reluctantly back to my feet.

"Here, Iverson, I'll defend your honour." Rich handed me his hot dog and reached for my controller.

I rolled my eyes and handed it over. Then I stared glumly at his half-eaten food while he made short work of the pins on the screen.

"There!" Rich blew on his controller, sharp-shooter style. "That's how it's done!"

JoJo stuck her tongue out at him. "I can still take you, Rich!"

Rich grinned. "You can try!"

"How's it going?" Dad stuck his head into the room.

"Pretty much normal to this point," I told him.

"Ah. JoJo beating you?"

"Thanks, Dad." I made a face at him. Another boost to my ego.

Dad laughed. "She reminds me of your mother."

"Mom beat you in everything, did she?"

"Everything."

I sighed.

"Anyway, can you shut things off for a while? Uncle Peter just radioed that there was a car coming up the drive."

"Anyone we know?"

"From his description, I would guess that it's Ms. Scott, coming to pay her weekly visit."

"Ugh!" Ms. Scott had proved to be a much better friend than either Dad or I had imagined when we first met her. But she was still rather . . . irritating. "Okay, Dad." I tossed my controller into the bin and reached for JoJo's.

JoJo handed it over. "You're just happy to have the beating stopped!"

"Too right," I muttered.

The doorbell rang. We all looked at each other. For some reason, I shivered.

Rich looked around. "I hear the sounds of doom!"

"I hear Todd's dad walking to the front door," JoJo said, grinning.

"Dooooooom!"

"So . . . D'you guys want to stay for this, or shall we find something else to do?" I was more than ready to find another place to be.

JoJo laughed. "Let's get out of here. I, for one, don't want to be around to listen to Ms. Scott's next plan for your dad's Essence.

"I know what I'd like to do . . ." Rich said. He grinned at us.

* * *

I'd lost count of how many times I'd done this. But each time just got more exciting and unbelievable. I opened my mouth to let out a yell of pure exhilaration.

"Screeeech!"

Oh, yeah.

I folded my wings and dropped toward the earth. It came at me at an alarming rate. I snapped my wings open and . . . stopped. Immediately.

And to think that I used to get queasy in an elevator.

I looked around, amazed once more at the absolute clarity of eagle sight. A couple of mice were nosing through the grass directly below me. I tilted my head to one side. Nope. Still didn't see the appeal. Maybe if one dunked them in chocolate sauce . . .? Nope. Not even then.

I looked further. A couple of figures were streaking across the stubble of the hayfield.

I swooped closer. Yep. A cougar and a grey wolf. Not two animals one would normally find in close proximity. I skimmed the air just over them.

"Screeeech!"

The grey wolf jumped a foot in the air.

If I had been able to laugh . . . well, I settled for a roll in the air.

The wolf leaped at me and snapped and I rowed my wings frantically to gain altitude.

I should note here that wolves can chuckle. I heard her as I struggled for height.

From a safe . . . well, a safe-er . . . distance, I watched the two of them race across the pasture. Wolf and cougar. Both fast. Both trying to outdistance the other.

The cougar leaped over the barbed wire fence just ahead of the wolf, but the wolf eeled between the sharp barbs and closed the distance.

The large cat's leaping advantage soon became obvious when the pair of them reached the haystacks. In one bound, it reached the top. Two strides took it to the far side and one more leap put it back on the ground.

The wolf paused for only a moment, then ducked its head and put on a burst of speed, skidding around the far corner of the stack. The cat nearly landed on it. Both animals paused. Startled.

Again, I opened my mouth to laugh. "Screeech!" Dang. I keep forgetting.

Finally, the two animals reached the frozen strip of ice that was the south fork of the Milk River.

They skidded to a halt and glared at each other, breathing heavily.

I landed just behind them. "Screeech!"

This time, all I got was a glance. The three of us sat there for a moment. Then, the wolf turned toward the ranch house and started off at a trot.

I leaped into the air and sailed ahead of them, landing on the house roof just as they reached the front steps.

The wolf pushed open the front door and disappeared inside. The cougar headed for the garage. I leaped from the roof into the air, then aimed for a thick patch of brush just at the edge of the lawn.

In a short time, the three of us were once more standing in my kitchen. I could hear voices coming from the front room.

Ugh. Ms. Scott giving my dad an earful, undoubtedly.

"Man, that is more exciting every time we do it!" Rick was rubbing his hands together as if they itched.

JoJo laughed. "Yeah. And if you could catch up to me, you'd really be doing something!"

"What?! I totally took you!"

"In your dreams, jock-boy, in your dreams."

Rich looked at me, disgusted. "Didn't I win, Iverson? Didn't I?"

I laughed. "I'm staying right out of this, Rich."

"Yeah, well, you'd be the best judge. You had height after all."

"And good eyesight," JoJo put in.

I laughed again. "And complete impartiality."

4

JoJo put her arm through mine. "Complete?"

I felt my face redden.

Rich laughed. "Yeah, I'd say that's the face of complete impartiality."

I rubbed an eye.

"So who won?" JoJo pressed.

"I . . . umm . . . really didn't see. I was too busy . . . flying."

"Nuts to that," Rich muttered, "you've been flying for months now. You're better than the real birds."

"Thanks for them kind words." I laughed.

"Oh, well. I guess there's always next time."

"Haven't you gotten it out of your system yet?" JoJo put her hands on her hips.

Rich shrugged. "Well, I never want to be a monkey again." He grinned. "But I'll never get enough of being a cougar!"

I rolled my eyes. "You're nuts."

His grin widened. "Maybe, Iverson, but it's a good kind of nuts!"

I snorted.

"C'mon, you have to admit, it's pretty exciting."

I grinned. "I don't have to admit anything."

Rich punched me playfully in the shoulder. "I'm just giving you a hard time, buddy," he walked over to the window and looked out over the frozen river. "Hard to believe it has been over six months now."

"Six months of peace and quiet," JoJo said.

"How about some hot chocolate?" I suggested.

Suddenly, Dad's raised voice reached us clearly. He sounded . . . irritated. "I'm sorry, Ms. Scott. You've been talking for half an hour. I have some work that I have to do and, though this is diverting, I really need to get back to it. So what is it that can I do for you?"

5

"Well, I think it's more a matter of what I can do for you, Dr. Iverson."

JoJo suddenly grabbed my hands and I looked down. I had managed to drop two full tablespoons of hot chocolate mix onto the cupboard. A cup was nowhere to be seen.

She rolled her eyes. "You're supposed to have something to hold the chocolate, T!" she pushed me away and took over.

I leaned back against the counter and folded my arms. "I'm better at this, anyway," I told her.

She laughed.

"What is it that you can do for me, Miranda?"

The sound of papers. Then, "My boss wants me to discuss the possibility of having you work with the military," she said at last.

"Military?" Dad sounded surprised.

"There is great potential for your discovery in the military, Dr. Iverson."

"Huh."

"Is that a good 'huh' or a bad one?"

"Just . . . huh."

JoJo silently thrust a mug of steaming cocoa into my hands and pushed me toward the table. Rich, already seated there, smiled up at us as he took a sip.

"So are you interested?"

"I will have to give this some thought, Miranda," Dad said slowly. "It's just . . . not something I would have considered."

"But it is a good idea. Think of the possibilities."

"I'm afraid I can't."

"What?! Animal abilities and instincts under the complete control of the military?"

"That sounds a bit . . ."

"Heightened senses and abilities. Strategy. Night work. The list could be endless."

"Yes, but remember that its effects only last for a short time."

"And that is something you could work on. In fact, that is my next proposal. That we move you to a real lab, with real equipment."

"And real guards patrolling the perimeter."

There was silence for several seconds. "Well, you have to understand, Dr. Iverson, that what you have discovered must be . . . protected . . . from anyone who might misuse it."

"Yes, we've already seen that happen."

"Exactly."

"So I improve the Essence for our military."

"Yes."

"Who would never misuse it."

Another silence.

Finally, "Dr. Iverson, I can't speak for everyone, I know but . . ."

"Exactly. You can't speak for everyone." The sound of a chair scraping. "Ms. Scott, my Essence is capable of turning men into animals. Literally. It could be misused as a terrible weapon."

"Well, we'd have to initiate controls . . ."

"Guard it."

"Well . . . yes."

"And guard me."

She was silent.

The chair scraped again. "Ms. Scott, I will have to think about this." Dad's voice moved toward the hall.

"But you will think about it?"

"Oh, I guarantee I'll do little else but think about it."

Ms. Scott's heels clicked on the floor in the front hall.

The door squeaked open.

"I probably didn't present my case very well, Dr. Iverson." Ms. Scott's voice sounded a bit desperate. "Please know that your Essence has caught the attention of some very important people . . ."

"I thought you were going to keep this under wraps," Dad was beginning to sound angry.

"Well, yes. I only told my boss," Ms. Scott admitted.

"And it's your boss who has come up with this new idea, all by himself?"

"Well . . . yes."

"Ms. Scott, why don't I believe you?"

"It's the truth, Dr. Iverson. I only told my boss. He's the one . . . He's . . ." her voice faded.

"Ah. He's the one who's been talking to those very important people."

"Well . . . yes."

"Thank you for stopping by, Ms. Scott. I promise I will give your proposal some thought."

"Thank you, Dr. Iverson." Ms. Scott sounded subdued. Something new for her.

The door closed.

Rich, JoJo and I looked at each other.

"So. Did you hear?" Dad had come into the kitchen behind me.

We nodded.

"What did you think of it?"

"I think you are right to be cautious, Dr. Iverson," JoJo spoke up. "From all the stories I have heard, once the military is involved . . ."

"You can kiss your control good-bye." Rich finished for her.

JoJo grinned at him. "For the first time, ever, Rich and I agree on something!"

"What are you going to do, Dad?"

Dad looked at me. "I don't know, son," he said. He sat at the end of the table and folded his hands together on top of it. "I created the Essence without really thinking about its possible uses." He sighed. "Short-sighted of me, I know, but there you go." His mouth twisted. "I really just wanted to carry on your mother's work."

JoJo set a cup of hot chocolate in front of him. "But now that other people know about it, you're going to have to come to a decision, Dr. Iverson."

Dad stared down into his mug. "You're right, as usual, JoJo," he said softly.

Chapter Two

"Jo!"

"It's tradition! You have to wear it!"

"But it's just an exhibition game!"

"It's still tradition."

"I look like a dork!"

Rich snorted. "I probably shouldn't point this out right now, Iverson, but you always look like a dork!"

"Thanks, Rich."

He grinned.

JoJo finished tying my tie. "There. You look smart."

"I shouldn't point this out . . ."

"Shut up, Rich."

Rich laughed and moved beside me in the mirror. "Actually, the tie looks good, T."

I tugged at it. "Doesn't look too dorky?"

"Well, don't get me started."

I rolled my eyes. "What am I saying?"

"So are you two ready?" JoJo had picked up her bag and stood waiting beside the door.

I grabbed my suit jacket. "As ready as I can be."

"Good, because the bus is waiting."

"It'll wait for the school's two star players!" Rich slapped me on the back.

I coughed and laughed. "Well one star player and his mascot," I corrected.

"Yeah, well, someday, I'm going to be as good as you!" Rich pushed the door open.

I laughed again. Rich was the school's top athlete. He had been lead scorer on the basketball floor since he had hit the seventh grade. Now, in grade nine, he was already playing centre with the high school team's first string. Tonight, because this was only an exhibition game, he was slumming with the juniors.

My accomplishments were far more modest. A late bloomer, I was only now playing in games where anyone was likely to see me.

I followed the two of them out to the long, yellow school bus, already crowded with players and cheerleaders.

"JoJo! Sit with us!" A tall girl with short-cropped blonde hair and bright, blue eyes was leaning out of one window.

JoJo laughed and shook her head. "Someone has to keep these two in line!" she said, punching both Rich and I in the shoulder.

The blonde girl laughed. "Well, just make sure you don't get injured keeping the peace. We need our centre for this game!"

JoJo laughed.

I watched her swing up the steps behind Rich. The two of them made a nice couple. Both tall and dark. Both athletic.

I wondered, for the millionth time, what JoJo was doing with me.

"T, hurry up!" Rich and JoJo had claimed an empty seat half-way up the aisle. JoJo squeezed over, pressing Rich into the window. "Here. There's plenty of room!"

I stared at the narrow spot and smiled. Cozy.

The bus ride to Lethbridge was fun. And noisy.

Some kids started singing, or rather shouting, and the rest of the bus joined in. The bus driver had to holler at us twice to tone it down.

We stepped off the bus at the Sportsplex and looked around.

Dozens of buses were parked along the centre of the parking lot. Hundreds of kids were milling around, more or less making their way toward one of the entrances.

A couple of Rich's former friends were standing nearby. I looked at them and they both turned away hurriedly.

"Looks like Jim and his friends still haven't forgotten their beating," JoJo whispered in my ear.

I smiled. Thrashing the school's former bullies was a very fond memory.

The Sportsplex was enormous. The main floor had been divided into two courts and games were already under way. The stands were crowded and I was surprised to see several people with clipboards sitting or standing on the lower tiers, obviously taking notes.

I pointed them out. "What are they? Reporters?"

Rich glanced at them. "Scouts," he said.

"What? Scouts?"

"Yeah. From colleges. They come to watch the high school teams play. Scout out the possible talent."

"Wow. No pressure!"

"Yeah, I suppose it can be pretty intimidating."

"Oooo! Intimidating! I didn't know you knew such long words!" JoJo grinned.

"Yeah. I'm copying you."

"Good example to follow." JoJo tossed her long hair back over her shoulder. "Well, I guess we'd better get suited up." She headed toward the girl's lockers. Several of her team members fell in behind her.

"Yeah. Unless we want to play in these clothes . . ." Rich waved a hand.

"Are you kidding? I don't even want to be *seen* in these clothes!" I followed him to the boy's side.

* * *

"Wow. JoJo's really good!"

I smiled proudly. "She really is."

12

"I guess I just never really noticed before."

I looked at Rich. Six months ago, he wouldn't have noticed anyone but himself. How different he was now.

"Get it! Get it!" he shouted.

JoJo scooped up the loose ball and tucked it neatly into the basket.

"And that, folks, is how it's done!" Rich grinned.

JoJo was playing really well. She made it look easy.

Later, as her team left the court in triumph, I saw two of the clipboard people approach her.

"Looks as though she is already attracting some attention."

Several male players from other teams were also hanging around.

Rich and I started down the bleachers.

JoJo spotted us. "Hey! Guys!" she waved.

As Rich and I joined her, she put her arms around my waist.

I grinned down at her. From the corner of my eye, I noticed that the other guys soon melted away.

"Wasn't I good? Wasn't I?"

"Were you playing?" I asked. "Dang! How did we miss that?"

"T!"

"You were perfect, Jo," Rich said.

"Ha! I knew you were watching!"

"She scored the winning basket!" The blonde girl from the bus had joined us.

"Oh, T, Rich, this is Jami."

"One of the not-the-best-players on the team," Jami grinned.

"Don't give me that," Rich said. "We were watching you!"

"You were? Watching me?"

"Watching *you*." Rich put just the slightest bit of emphasis on the last word.

I raised my eyebrows and looked at JoJo.

She was grinning. She leaned closer. "I've been trying to get those two together for months," she whispered in my ear. "What do you think?"

I looked at Rich who was obviously interested.

Then at Jami, who was more than interested.

I nodded. "Looks good," I whispered back.

JoJo's grin widened.

We left the two of them together and walked over to the concession stand.

A short time later, Rich and Jami joined us.

JoJo laughed. "Huh. We thought you'd forgotten we existed."

Both Rich and Jami flushed pink.

"We'd better get going, T," Rich said. "We're up next." He turned to Jami. "See you later?"

"Count on it!" Jami said.

Rich and I headed for our assigned court.

Rich looked back and waved. "So what do you think of her?"

I stared at him. He was grinning like an idiot.

"I'd say she's obviously just right for you."

"I think so, too."

"Hey you two! Get over here!" The coach was standing in the centre of a large knot of boys, looking at us.

"Sorry, coach." We quickly joined the others.

* * *

Rich didn't play with his usual skill. Once, he even stumbled. I saw his eyes stray into the crowd. I glanced up. JoJo and Jami were sitting there.

All was explained. The mighty Rich. Felled by a pair of blue eyes. I smiled. The cougar was human after all.

We lost our game. Narrowly, but a loss just the same. Dejected, we left the court.

"What happened to you, Rich?" one of the players moved up beside us. "You were playing like a girl out there!"

Rich looked at him. "If I'd been playing like a girl, we would have won, Dudley. Or didn't you see the girl's game just ahead of ours?"

Dudley slouched off.

Then JoJo and Jami were standing in front of us. "Little off your game, Rich?" JoJo asked, grinning.

Rich turned bright red. "A little," he mumbled.

Jami laughed and linked her arm with his. "We all have off days, Rich."

"But it's especially bad when we're trying to impress someone," JoJo laughed.

Rich just shook his head.

"Get used to it, buddy," I told him.

He glanced at me, then at Jami. "Suffering never looked so good." He grinned crookedly.

The seating arrangements for the ride home were a bit different than they had been on the trip out. Rich and Jami took a seat directly behind JoJo and me. Every time I glanced back at them, they had their heads together, talking.

JoJo saw where I was looking. "Looks good, doesn't it?"

"It does. Rich has come a long way."

She slid down in her seat. "I think of how lost and frightened he was that day in the park," she whispered. "He had truly hit bottom."

"And I also remember his first day back at school afterwards, when everyone else was treating him like a leper, and you went over and befriended him."

JoJo smiled. "Well, after everything we'd been through, I just thought . . . well . . . that we should stick together."

"And you were right. As usual."

"Get used to it, T."

I grinned. "I plan to."

* * *

A strange car was parked in the driveway when I reached home later that evening. I frowned. Now who could this be?

Voices in the front room. I dropped my backpack on the kitchen table and threw my sports bag into the laundry room. I stopped in the doorway.

Dad was talking with Ms. Scott and a short, heavy man with a fringe of iron-grey hair around a shiny bald spot.

Dad turned as I entered.

"Oh, Todd. How did it go?" He turned to the man. "This is my son, Todd. He was playing in a basketball exhibition game this afternoon in Lethbridge."

I shrugged. "We lost."

"Oh, son, I'm sorry to hear that."

"It's okay. There was a reason." Yeah. A good reason. Our star player was twitterpated.

"Did you have fun?"

"Yeah, I really did."

"Well, that's all that counts."

"JoJo's team won," I offered.

"Well that's good to hear."

"Yeah, they pretty much trounced the team they were playing."

"Good. Good." Dad seemed . . . preoccupied.

I decided I'd interrupted his business long enough. "Well, I think I'll go into the kitchen and get something to eat." I looked at the three of them. "Can I get anything for you? Juice? Water?"

"Thanks, Todd, I didn't even think . . ." Dad turned to the other two. "Can we offer you anything?"

"Oh," the man answered. "Thanks, but no. Ms. Scott and I will be leaving soon."

I nodded and headed for the kitchen, loosening my tie as I went.

Dad had left a plate of dinner for me in the fridge. I popped the plate into the microwave and rummaged for a fork and knife.

"So what do you think of our proposal?" The man in the next room was talking.

"Like I told Ms. Scott, I will have to think about it."

"It'll make you a rich man, Dr. Iverson. And how many scientists ever accomplish that?"

"If you're just going to get insulting . . ."

"We're just trying to help you see the advantages to our proposal," Ms. Scott broke in soothingly.

"Well, I'm not interested in being rich," Dad said testily.

"We understand. But Todd . . ."

"Leave my son out of this."

"I'm sorry, Dr. Iverson." Ms. Scott said. "I was only thinking of his future."

"As am I."

"Education and such."

"I can afford to educate my son!" Dad was really getting irritated.

"Well, you have my card." The rustling of papers. The scrape of a chair.

"I do."

"Please give us a call when you've made your decision," the man said. There was a pause. "I don't have to tell you that this offer has a time limit."

"No, you don't have to tell me anything."

"Yes. Well, we'd better be going."

The man stopped just inside the front door. "I'll be looking forward to hearing from you, Dr. Iverson."

"Fine." Dad closed the door behind them.

The microwave binged. I grabbed the plate and carried it over to the table.

"Well, that was an experience." Dad had come into the kitchen from the front hall.

"What was it all about? And who was that guy with Ms. Scott."

"Didn't I introduce you?" Dad shook his head. "I'm sorry, son. I guess he just had me so

rattled I wasn't thinking straight."

"That's okay, Dad. So . . . who was he?"

"Ms. Scott's boss. Whitaker or something like that . . ." Dad pulled a business card from his pocket. "Yeah. Whitaker."

"So he's the chief spy?"

Dad half-smiled. "Well, the head of their department at any rate."

"Yeah, he doesn't really look like the James Bond type."

Dad laughed. "Definitely not!"

"So what did they want?" I speared a piece of chicken and stuffed it into my mouth.

Dad sat down. "They want the Essence."

"What are they going to do with it?"

"They want to market it to the military."

"Well, that doesn't seem too bad. Our military could probably use it."

"Not to our military, son. To the highest bidding military."

I stared at him. "So he'll, like, shop it around. Take bids?"

"Yes. Take bids."

"But then every military organization in the world, good and bad, will know about it. Will come running"

Dad nodded sadly.

"Not good, Dad."

"I know."

"So what are you going to do?"

"I just can't decide. I think of the money, of course."

"Dad, we don't need the money."

He smiled. "Well, not now, but maybe later . . ."

"Not later, either."

"And then I think it might help. Maybe save a few lives. And I wonder if I really have the right to withhold it."

"Dad, one thing I do know is that you always have the right to make your own decisions."

He nodded. "Part of me knows that."

"But the other part?"

He sighed. "When I see the cost in human lives and suffering in places like Iraq or Afghanistan, I wonder if the Essence could possibly help. Possibly be the edge we need to resolve these conflicts."

I was silent.

Dad stood up. "Well, I'll just have to give it some more thought." He went to the garage door. "Finish up and get yourself into bed, okay, son?"

I nodded. "No worries, Dad."

He smiled tiredly and left.

* * *

The moon was shining in my window, making a sharp outline on the carpet. Shadows dimmed it slightly. I sat up and looked outside. The wind had risen and was blowing the clouds across it.

I got up and walked over to the window, leaning my head against the cold glass.

From somewhere outside, I heard the long, mournful wail of a wolf. Another answered. Then movement caught my eye.

A large, black cat appeared from under the trees, running hard, its large paws barely seeming to touch the ground. It streaked past me across the yard and headed into the hay field.

Dad was working out his problems in his own way. Both mentally and physically.

I smiled. For a moment, I wondered who would have won if Dad's panther had been racing Rich and JoJo. I shrugged. I'd probably never know.

I went back to bed.

Chapter Three

The bus rumbled off down the drive, leaving a cloud of dust behind it.

Jami watched it go. Then she turned, put her hands on her hips, and looked at Rich, JoJo and I. "Okay. I'm here," she said. "Now what's the big secret?"

"Well . . . I . . . ." Rich was obviously lost for words. He swallowed and tried again, "I . . ."

JoJo laughed. "You're not going to get it out, are you, Rich?"

Rich turned a brilliant shade of red.

"It's okay," Jami soothed, reaching for his hand. "You don't have to tell me if you don't want to."

I snorted. "Oh, c'mon, Rich, spit it out!"

JoJo glanced around. "Maybe we'd better go somewhere else," she suggested.

Rich nodded. "Yeah. Somewhere a little less . . . public."

I frowned. "Who is going to hear us?"

"Well . . . your dad?"

"My dad? The guy who knows more about this than we do?! And who would have a hard time listening in . . . from Lethbridge!"

Dad had gone to Lethbridge with Uncle Peter and Aunt Bett. They were planning to have supper in the city before they headed home. As it was a Friday, I had decided that it would be a good opportunity to invite my friends over.

And Rich had decided it would be a good opportunity to let Jami in on our little not-so-secret secret.

JoJo laughed. "He's got a point, Rich."

"Well, I'd feel a bit more comfortable if we went somewhere a bit more secluded."

"All right," I grinned. Sometimes Rich was just so much fun to tease. "Let's go to Dad's lab."

"Your dad has a lab?" Jami's eyes had gotten big.

"A really scary one with blinking lights and electrical sparks and dripping beakers," JoJo said. "And deadly creatures lurking behind locked doors."

"Really?"

"She's just scaring you," Rich said quickly. "It's just a normal lab like the one at school."

"But useful," I put in. "Work actually gets done there."

JoJo laughed. "Yeah. Actually, not like the one at school at all!"

I turned and led the way through the front door and down the stairs.

JoJo and Jami each sat on one of the tall stools at a large, metal table. Rich and I stood opposite them.

"Okay. This private enough?" JoJo asked.

Rich nodded. He looked at Jami. "I'm sure you've heard the stories about Todd's dad by now."

"Boy, have I ever," Jami grinned. "They just get keep getting more and more fantastic."

"Sooo . . . what have you heard?"

"Oh, stupid things like Dr. Iverson's got a nasty lab here where he experiments on animals and people. Turning the one into the other and vice-versa." She glanced around. "I guess we can scratch the 'nasty lab' part, at least."

I, too, looked around. A lab less likely to harbour anything nasty couldn't be found. This room was brightly lit and very tidy. Equipment was arranged on tables and cupboards, neatly hooded or shrouded. The overall impression was of cleanliness and order.

"Well, I have to tell you that some of those stories are true," Rich went on.

"What?!" Jami sat up straight.

"Oh, not the nasty bits about experimenting on people," Rich went on hurriedly, "but the parts where he works with animals."

Jami just stared at him. "Oh."

JoJo laughed. "I think you'd better explain, Rich, before she gets the wrong idea."

"Too late!" I put in.

"You . . . you tell her, Todd," Rich said.

I grinned. "Happy to, Rich," I said. I turned to Jami. "So, Jami, what he says about working with animals is true. He and my mom have been following that particular course of study since University."

"Your mom?"

"She died when I was really young."

"Oh," she said again.

"Anyway, Dad has been trying to find out just exactly what makes an animal an animal."

"And he has done it!" JoJo broke in. "He has isolated the specific genes that make an animal unique."

"And not only was he able to isolate them, he was then able to use them to create a serum. An . . . Essence that, when ingested, allows a person to actually . . . become that animal."

Jami was staring at me, her mouth a little open. "Become . . .?"

"Yes, Jami," JoJo said. "It really works. We've all done it."

"Done what?"

"Become animals."

"But don't freak out or anything," Rich said quickly. "It's not dangerous or anything."

"No, you retain your own thoughts and everything," JoJo put in. "The only thing that changes is your appearance."

"And your abilities," I said.

Jami was still staring. "So what you are telling me is that you get to turn yourself into a . . . oh, a bear or something . . . but you can still think and stuff?"

"Exactly!" Rich said, enthusiastically.

"Are you all right with this, Jami?" JoJo asked.

"I'm not . . ." Jami said slowly. "You're sure it's not dangerous?"

"Absolutely," I told her. "I, myself have been several animals."

"Like what?"

"Well, a finless porpoise was my first."

"You might have heard about that," JoJo said.

Jami shook her head.

"The flood? When the guy was rescued by some sort of animal."

Jami caught her breath. "That was you?!"

I grinned. "That was me. I almost drowned doing it, but that was me."

"Huh. I just figured some guys had been hitting the bottle at work."

I laughed. "A lot of people thought that."

"So what else?"

"Well, I've been a pig and a goat." I grinned. "I've even been a chicken."

"That was fun," JoJo put in.

"But a chicken is . . . little. You're . . . bigger." She frowned doubtfully.

"You have to understand that the change happens on a sub-atomic level," JoJo said.

"Yes, our atoms are made up of matter. But they are also made up of air. And air can be manipulated," I told her.

"In creating the cells of the animal, our cells are . . . well . . . for want of a better term, shrunk or expanded, depending on the shape we assume," JoJo went on.

"We end up with the same number of cells as in our own bodies, just . . . different sizes."

"And shapes," JoJo laughed.

"Huh." Jami still looked confused.

"But you could be like me and ignore all of that and focus on what's important. Becoming an animal!" Rich broke in.

Jami shrugged. "I guess," she said. She looked at me. "So, Todd, which animal do you prefer?"

I looked at JoJo. She grinned and nodded.

"Well mostly, I prefer to be an eagle," I told her.

"An eagle?" Jami stared at me. "Like the one that appears whenever we have a football game?"

"That would be Todd," Rich said.

"Wow." Her face cleared and she smiled. "That is so cool!"

Rich let out his breath. I looked at him. Had he been holding it this whole time?

"I've been a panther and a wolf," JoJo said. "I really wanted to try the horse Essence, but Todd says it's still 'under construction', or something like that."

"Yeah, Dad still hasn't worked all of the kinks out of it yet."

Jami turned to Rich. "So what have you been?"

"Well . . . mostly . . ."

"Rich has only been one thing," JoJo said. "A cougar."

"I like cougars," Rich said, defensively.

"I love cougars!" Jami said enthusiastically. "I would so love to be a cougar!"

Rich grinned. "So, Jami, would you care to try . . ."

"Could I?"

"It's totally safe," JoJo said.

Rich held up a vial. Jami took it and looked at it.

"It's so tiny," she said. "Are you sure that this is all I need?"

"Very sure," Rich grinned. "The voice of experience speaking."

"So what do I need to do?"

"Come with me," JoJo said. "I'm afraid the first thing you have to do is get naked." She looked at Rich and me and grinned. "And that's something we don't want to do with these two Neanderthals looking on."

Jami made a face. "Too right," she said, her cheeks pink with excitement.

The girls disappeared in the direction of the stairs.

"I thought that went well," Rich said.

"Yeah."

"So, shall we?"

A thought suddenly struck me. I laughed.

"What is it?"

"Well, I just realized something."

"Yeah?"

"Having the Essence brings a whole new meaning to the phrase, 'let's get changed'."

Rich laughed and nodded.

* * *

A panther and a cougar were already out on the grass when Rich, also a cougar, and I, a leopard this time, emerged a few minutes later.

The cougar was running in circles and leaping into the air.

The panther was sitting, watching her.

The cougar bounded over to Rich, making tiny, excited hops in front of him. He nodded and spun around, heading toward the hay field. The other cougar wasn't far behind.

I looked at the panther. She moved over beside me and bumped me with her nose. Then the two of us took off after our friends.

For several minutes, the four of us ran back and forth across the hay field, chasing, racing and challenging each other to greater and greater feats.

Jami easily matched Rich's trick of reaching the top of the hay stack in one bound, then went one step further and actually cleared the stack in one bound. Rich stopped where he was and stared at her. Then shook his head.

I looked over at JoJo to see her reaction.

She hadn't noticed. She was looking toward the east.

I followed her gaze.

A slight glow could be seen on the cliff top across the river, east of the ranch site.

Fire!

Without pausing, the two of us set out at top speed for the bridge.

In moments, we were across it and streaking up the hill.

Then JoJo suddenly left the road and bounded off toward the cliff top, clearing the fence with a smooth, effortless leap.

The light brightened. We quickened our pace.

I really hadn't considered what a couple of large cats could do about a prairie fire. I just knew how dangerous and deadly a grass fire could be. My instinctive thought was to reach it before it got too big and stop it from spreading.

We skidded to a stop just over a little rise.

In a shallow swale, three figures were seated comfortably around a campfire, obviously enjoying a last cup of coffee before turning in for the night. Large packs

27

had been dropped just outside the fire's glow, and their bedrolls were already laid out. Long rifles in holsters lay on the ground beside each of them. Their horses were hobbled nearby.

Hunters.

It was the season and I probably shouldn't have been too surprised. Our pastures offered prime grazing for deer, elk and antelope, and there were very few homes or settlements way out here. Hunters were common.

JoJo and I froze, but the horses were downwind from us and they began to stamp and move about nervously.

Damn, they could smell us.

The hunters lifted their heads and looked at their mounts.

The horses were looking toward us, ears up. One of them snorted. That seemed to be the signal for all three to begin to blow loudly.

Two of the hunters ran to the horses, grabbing for halters and trying to find leads. The third hunter rose slowly to his feet, his face turned in our direction. He had his gun uncovered and in his hands.

I nudged JoJo and the two of us started to back slowly away.

Just then, Rich and Jami came up behind us at full speed. One of them ploughed right into me, turned a summersault over my back and landed awkwardly between me and the fire.

"What the . . .!" The hunter never finished his sentence, merely lifted his rifle and fired.

A feline scream of pain. The cat went down.

Rich or Jami. I ran toward it, feeling worse than sick, but a second cat got there ahead of me and nudged the injured one with its nose.

The wounded cat moved and my heart gave a wild leap as it stood up.

Then a streak of darker black whizzed past me toward the fire.

"Don! Greg! Cougars! A bunch of them!"

Another shot rang wildly. Then a third.

"Watch out, Stu, you idiot! You're going to hit . . .!"

I watched in disbelief as JoJo shot over the campfire toward the horses.

The horses went crazy, bucking and kicking. One of them managed to jerk his lead from the numb fingers of a hunter and, hobbles and all, took off at a clumsy hop-run across the prairie. The other two plunged and leapt crazily.

I looked back at Rich and Jami. The wounded one was limping badly but making progress away from the fire and into the cover of the dark, the other close beside it.

I glanced over my shoulder to where I had seen JoJo. She had completely disappeared.

The horses were still snorting nervously and obviously contemplating the merits of the nearest far-away place, but the hunters had clamped hands over their noses and they were starting to quiet down.

The hunter with the gun was now peering at the spot where JoJo had last been.

I was just wondering if I should try to go back and find her when a large black shape appeared out of the darkness beside me. I leaped a foot into the air and JoJo gave me a bat with one large paw. Then she turned to catch up with the others. I fell in behind her.

As quietly as we could, we followed the ridge down toward the road. Getting past the fence was a bit more awkward this time, but we finally managed to squeeze our wounded friend between the lower two wires. Soon we were across the bridge and running through the hay field.

The wounded cat seemed to be moving better and I was more than relieved. By the time we had reached the lights of the house, its limp had all but disappeared.

I charged straight through the front door and the hall, skidding to a stop in the kitchen.

The other three joined me. JoJo was examining the shoulder of one of the cougars. It was wet with fresh blood, but didn't seem to be oozing now.

I moved closer. Yes, it had bled quite a bit. The leg and paw were both soaked in it. I looked for a wound, but all I could see was a small . . . trail . . . through the thick fur.

I sat back and shook my head.

JoJo looked at me and . . . shrugged. Then she tipped her head toward the bathroom. The wounded cougar nodded and the two of them disappeared into the hall.

It was only then that I realized it was Jami who had been wounded.

Great.

I headed for the basement with Rich right behind me.

JoJo was standing beside the fridge when we emerged a few minutes later.

"Where's Jami?" Rich demanded.

"She's taking a bath," JoJo said.

"Is she all right?"

"She's fine."

"How can that be?" Rich sank into a chair. "My heart stopped when she went down. I thought that hunter had killed her!"

"As did we all," JoJo said. She shook her head. "I guess she wasn't as badly hurt as we thought."

Rich rubbed one hand over his face. "I don't understand," he said.

"That was the most amazing thing I have ever experienced in my life!" Jami came into the room.

Rich's gloomy expression disappeared. "You're all right? You really enjoyed it?"

"I'm fine. And it was fantastic!" She grimaced. "Well, apart from the whole 'getting shot' scenario."

"Where did you get shot?" Rick moved over to her.

"Here." Jami pulled the collar of her T-shirt to one side, disclosing a red welt about 6 inches long, just below her collarbone.

"Wow!" He frowned and reached out to touch the spot gently. "It looks like it only grazed you."

"Well, it felt a whole lot worse than a graze," Jami said, grinning. "I thought the bullet had shot my whole chest off."

JoJo walked over and examined the wound. "Huh. It really doesn't look too bad," she said. She touched it with gentle fingers. "In fact, it looks like little more than a bruise." She shook her head. "I don't understand it. From the amount of blood on you when we got back here . . ."

"I know. Weird, isn't it?" Jami shrugged. She looked at her shoulder. "Look. It's not even as red as it was."

The wound was definitely disappearing.

"There's something you don't see every day," I said.

JoJo laughed. "That's the theme of this place."

I frowned. "I think we've just opened a whole new can of worms."

JoJo looked at me and raised her eyebrows. "Are you thinking what I'm thinking?" she asked quietly.

I moved closer to her. "Possibly." My voice was just above a whisper.

"That the new matrix gives the cells advanced healing properties."

I glanced at Jami. "And that the condition exists even when the person has changed back. At least for a time."

JoJo nodded.

"I'll have to discuss this with Dad."

"Good."

"What are you guys talking about so quietly?"

I looked up. Rich and Jami were staring at us.

"Just discussing Jami's wound."

"Well enough of that," Jami said. "I want to talk about being a cougar!"

Rich was easily distracted. "Isn't it the greatest?!" he asked.

"The best experience of my life!" Jami said. "Amazing! Stupendous! Really, really exciting! So . . . you guys do this all of the time?"

"Well, as often as we can," JoJo said. "Todd's dad keeps a pretty close eye on us, just in case."

"In case of what?"

"You have to realize that the Essence is still in its experimental stages," I told her.

"And needs to be monitored," JoJo put in.

"So Dad keeps track of what we take and how often."

"So he knew that you were going to bring me out here tonight?"

"Of course," Rich said. "He was the one who gave us the vials."

"I think I like your dad."

"Me, too," I said.

"Well, I hate to sound mundane, but is there anything to eat? I'm starving!"

"Near-death experiences will do that to you," Rich laughed.

"Let's see what we can find," I said, opening the fridge.

We spent the rest of the evening eating and playing games.

"This all seems so normal," Jami said later, "after . . ."

"Yeah, everything seems tame after a dose of Essence," Rich said. He sighed. "But that's the price we pay for a few minutes of heart-stopping action."

"Exactly," JoJo agreed. "Everything in moderation."

"You sound like my mom," Rich grinned.

"Then she must sound really, really smart." JoJo made a face at him.

Rich snorted.

Lights flashed through the window and a car horn honked.

"Oh-oh, there's my dad," JoJo said, glancing at her watch. "I had no idea it was so late. I guess we'd better go." She looked around at the dirty dishes and clutter and made a face. "I'm really sorry that we didn't help you get this cleaned up, T."

"Don't worry about it, Jo," I told her. "I didn't want to waste any of the evening washing dishes."

She gave me a hug. "You're the best, T. The very best."

"Ummm . . . glad you noticed, Jo."

"C'mon, guys. Dad hates to be kept waiting." JoJo dove out the door into the darkness.

Rich and Jami grabbed their coats.

"Thanks, Todd," Jami said. "It was a . . . an amazing evening!"

"Glad you enjoyed it, Jami."

"More than enjoyed it, but that'll do for now!" She followed JoJo.

Rich grinned and smacked me on the shoulder. "Thanks, buddy," he said. "Let's do this again!"

I grimaced and glared at him, rubbing my shoulder. "Anytime, buddy. My pleasure."

He laughed. Then he, too disappeared into the night.

* * *

I was just finishing clearing up when Dad got back. He sighed and pulled off his coat.

33

"You okay, Dad?"

"Fine, Son." He sat at the table. "How did things go here?"

"Really well. Well, mostly well."

"Problems?"

"Well . . ." I was stumped. It's not every day that you and your friends turn into giant cats. Surprise some hunters. Get shot at and wounded. Come home and make cocoa and play games. Not your normal evening . . .

And where to start? "Jami really enjoyed turning into a cougar," I managed at last.

"Oh?"

"Yeah. She was pretty enthusiastic and already talking about 'next time'."

"Well, that's good."

I sighed. "Dad, I'll have to tell you about what happened . . ."

Dad was looking at me. I could see alarm in his eyes.

"It was nothing . . . well, turned out to be nothing . . ." I ran out of words.

"You'd better explain, son."

"Yeah. Well. We got changed and were having great fun running back and forth across the hay field . . ."

"Go on."

"Well, JoJo noticed a glow up on the top of the cliff. On the east side."

"Fire?!"

"Don't worry, Dad, it was only a campfire. Hunters."

"Oh."

"But we didn't realize that until we got there."

"You went up there?"

"Yeah, well, all we saw was a glow and we had to investigate."

Dad nodded. "I guess I can see that."

"Anyway, Rich and Jami followed us and one of them ran into me and ended up between me and the fire."

"That doesn't sound too good."

"It wasn't. One of the hunters shot it and it went down."

Dad went pale and caught his breath. "Please tell me that this ends all right."

I sat down. "Everything's fine, Dad."

He shook his head. "So . . .?"

"JoJo ran straight through their camp, over the fire."

Dad put his face into his hands and moaned aloud.

"They were so concerned about her that they stopped watching the rest of us and we were able to get the wounded one out of the camp and into the cover of the dark."

Dad lifted his head. "So they are here?!" He got to his feet. "Where are they?" He pulled off his jacket. "I'll need to collect some bandages, suture . . ." he continued to mumble to himself.

"Dad. Dad! They're not here!"

He turned back to me. "What?"

"No. We had a great evening and JoJo's dad picked them up a while ago."

Dad sat back down, heavily. "Great evening?" He frowned.

"Please let me finish."

He nodded, folding his hands together on the table.

"JoJo joined us as we ran toward the road. The hunters never were able to follow her. She didn't get injured at all."

"Well, that's good, but what about the one who did?"

I paused a moment. "Well, this is where it gets a bit . . . complicated."

Dad stared at me.

"You see, the one who got hit was Jami."

35

"Oh, fantastic . . ."

"But she's fine."

Again, he stopped speaking and stared at me. "So they missed?"

"No, actually, it was quite serious. As nearly as we can tell, the bullet passed along her chest here," I indicated on myself, "ploughing a deep groove, but not actually entering the body."

"Okay." Dad's voice had been reduced to a whisper.

"At first, she bled quite a lot. In fact, we had a hard time getting her to the fence beside the road. But once we got past there, she seemed to be moving better. As we crossed the hay field, she was keeping up, no problem."

Dad was staring again.

"By the time we got back here, the bleeding had stopped and the wound was almost completely healed over."

He blinked. "So you're telling me . . . What are you telling me?"

"Well, Dad, I . . . well, JoJo and I . . . think that the Essence gives people regenerative abilities."

He was silent for a full minute. "Huh," he said at last.

"After Jami had a bath, she came out here and showed us her wound. It was just a red mark on her skin. And as we watched, it got . . . less red."

"Huh."

"Is that all you can say?"

He nodded.

I grinned. "The great scientist."

He shook his head. "The very unremarkable scientist who just got his teeth kicked in."

"Dad, in no way could you be considered unremark . . ."

"So, you're saying that this wound was quite deep," he broke in.

"Yeah. I mean, I didn't actually lay eyes on it. It would have been quite hard to see through Jami's fur and in the dark, but from the amount of blood she lost . . ."

He nodded. "But by the time she showed you the wound, it was healed."

"Yeah."

"How long would this have been?"

"Couldn't have been more than about 10 minutes."

"Huh." Dad scratched an eyebrow.

"So what do you think?"

"I really don't know what to think," he said.

"Yeah, I know what you mean."

He sat up and looked at me. "Remember when I was scratched by Rich's uncle?"

"How can I forget?" It was only one of the scariest moments in my life.

"And the scratches disappeared remarkably quickly . . ."

"Did they?" I scrunched up my forehead in thought. "I remember trying to re-bandage your arm and thinking that they didn't look too bad."

"Trust me, son, by the next morning, when I looked at them, I wondered why the doctor had even bothered with stitches. There was hardly a mark on my arm."

"Weird."

He rubbed his hand over his face and frowned. "Well, this gives me something more to think about," he said. He looked at me again. "How was Jami with all of this?"

"She handled it really well."

"Yeah, you said she was already talking about next time . . ."

"Yeah. She was a real trooper."

"And do you think she will talk?"

I shook my head. "Not at all. JoJo and Rich really stressed the importance of keeping quiet."

"But she was injured . . ."

"Yeah, well, that was just one more exciting event in the whole exciting evening."

He sighed. "That's good." He put his head into his hands.

"Dad?"

He looked up. "I've got to figure out what to do, Son. And now you and your friends have provided yet another wrinkle."

"Sorry, Dad."

"Peter, Bett and I have spent hours tonight," he sighed, "talking about it."

"So what have you decided?"

He looked toward the darkened window. "Well," he said finally, "if the Essence has to be used for something, I would much rather it was used for good."

"That goes without saying."

"Yes. So, I think I would rather turn it over to our military than risk Whitaker's 'auction to the highest bidder'."

I sat back. "Well, there are some pretty rich terrorists who could pay a lot for it."

"Exactly. And if they got hold of it, who knows what they could use it for."

I nodded. "I think that's the right course, Dad."

"It's the only course, son. Give it to our military and let them use it. And let them try to protect it."

"They're probably a bit more experienced at that sort of thing than we are."

Dad smiled, tiredly. "I sure hope so, Son."

Chapter Four

A dusty, black Ford Taurus stood in the driveway. A soldier, dressed in the green fatigues of the United States army, stood beside it, his head turned toward me. Dark glasses covered his eyes.

"Hello, son," he called.

"Um . . . hello?"

He came toward me, right hand outstretched. "I'm Major Egleson."

I shifted the pail of eggs I held into my other hand and reached out to shake his. "Nice to meet you."

He glanced down at my eggs and smiled, then tossed his head toward the house. "My boss is just in talking to your boss."

I glanced at the car once more, then back to the soldier. "Oh." Sparkling repartee as usual, Iverson, I congratulated myself.

Major Egleson returned to his car. "Carry on, kiddo."

I nodded at him and went into the garage, then through into the kitchen. I could immediately hear the rumble of voices from the front room.

"I'm afraid I really don't see your point." Dad's voice.

A mumble, too low for me to make out.

"No, I don't see the advantage. They could still be injured. Still die."

Another mumble.

"I'm sorry General. I simply don't agree. It wouldn't make them invincible. Only sharpen senses and abilities. Oh, I know that any enhancement could help, theoretically, but it wouldn't ensure their safety."

"But that is exactly what we need, Dr. Iverson." Now I could hear the voice. Its owner must have turned toward the door. "Sharper eyes. Heightened senses. All of these could give them the edge they need. They'd be able to avoid the things that have been killing them."

"No one wants the killing to stop more than I do, General. But what I'm saying is that they'd still be mortal. Vulnerable. Heightened senses and abilities might make them . . . reckless."

The general chuckled. "They are already reckless, son. That's why they are in my army." His voice changed. Softened. "I want to keep them in my army. Alive in my army."

There was a pause.

"But I'd have to work from your lab?"

"We'll need to keep you close. Monitor your progress."

"I'll have to tell you that any progress gained in research would be nullified by my lost freedom."

"What are you talking about? You'd still be a free man, Iverson."

"You know as well as I do that the moment the military gets its hands on something top secret, all of the walls come up. And the locks go on."

"I think you've been watching too many Jack Ryan movies."

"Are you trying to tell me that if I agree to work with the military, you'll allow me to stay here on my ranch and work downstairs in my lab and have complete freedom?"

"Well, of course there will have to be changes."

"Ah. Now we come to it."

"Well, you can see yourself the need for security."

"Security. Code word for locked up."

"Well, once the word got out, you'd have to be protected."

"And that's the exact reason why I don't want the word to get out."

"I'm afraid it's too late for that, Iverson," the voice said quietly.

I set the pail of eggs on the counter and went to the doorway of the front room.

Dad was sitting on a straight chair in front of the couch, staring at the short man in a US army officer's uniform standing with his back to the picture window.

The officer looked at me. "Ah. And who is this?"

Dad turned. I was surprised at how red his face was. Dad hardly ever lost his temper.

I guess this was one of the 'hardlys'.

"Oh. Todd." Dad rose and glanced back at the man in front of the window. "General, I'd like you to meet my son, Todd. Son, this is General Dune."

The general moved forward and offered his hand. The sun winked off four gold stars on his left shoulder as he moved. "Pleasure, son," he said.

I mumbled something.

"So, your only son?"

"My only family, General."

"Ah." The general picked up a folder from the couch and tucked a gold-braided hat under his left arm. "Well, I guess we've talked enough for today."

"Yes, we definitely have."

"I just want you to think about my proposal, Iverson," The general glanced at me. "It could help a lot of people."

Dad said nothing, just followed the general to the front door and closed it behind him.

He leaned back against it. "Man, if ever I've wanted to throttle someone . . .!"

"You okay, Dad?"

He was pinching the bridge of his nose, his chin almost touching his chest.

Dad took a deep breath and levered himself away from the door. "I will be, son." He reached out and ruffled

41

my hair. "Ready for supper?" He started toward the kitchen and I followed.

The doorbell rang and Dad spun around and glared at the door. Then he sighed and pulled it open.

"Hi, Hank!"

"Amy! Am I glad to see you!"

Amy Linden stepped inside and was immediately swept into a hug.

I raised my eyebrows. This was certainly a different greeting than the indomitable Ms. Scott had received a couple of days ago. I snorted quietly. And obviously way warmer than the General had gotten.

Dad and Amy had been seeing quite a bit of each other since the incident at the bank when she had come to our rescue. But this was first time she had ever made the drive to the ranch by herself.

Dad freed the woman, but kept an arm around her shoulders. They both turned toward me.

"Hello, Todd," Amy smiled, green eyes twinkling.

"Hi, Amy."

"We were just about to get some supper," Dad told her. "Would you like to join us?"

"Nothing I'd like better," Amy said. "And maybe I'll be able to tell you what brings me out here."

Dad looked at her. "You mean it's not me?" He waggled his eyebrows.

I was reminded, suddenly, of the tent-caterpillar epidemic a couple of years before. Smooth, Dad.

Amy laughed. "Okay, you were part of the reason."

"Only part?"

She laughed again. "C'mon, let's feed you. And me." She smiled up at me. "And definitely Todd."

* * *

I had never experienced making a meal with anyone but my dad. Amy made it fun. As I set the table, I watched the two of them. They seemed to bump into each other a lot. They must have enjoyed it though, because they certainly laughed.

In no time, we were sitting down to chicken fettuccine and salad. For some reason, the food tasted even better than usual.

Dad and Amy laughed a lot and dad was in top story-telling form. But something in Amy's eyes told me that the real reason for her appearance had not come out yet.

Finally, she pushed away her dessert plate and folded her hands together on the table. "I need to tell you about some things I've been hearing, Hank."

Dad sobered immediately. He glanced at me. "Is it all right for Todd . . ."

"Certainly, Todd needs to hear this." She took a deep breath. "Roddy Walters has been doing some talking from his prison cell."

"Talking from prison was always that family's strong suit," Dad muttered.

"Yes, well, he has had some pretty interesting things to say, and I'm afraid that there are some people who are starting to listen."

"Like what?"

"Well, he has been talking about this magic potion that allows people to turn into animals. He's saying that it's these 'people/animals' who were robbing the banks and that he had nothing to do with it."

"Does he explain how he knows about this? Or how he got into the cage in place of the bear?" Dad asked.

"Naked?" I had to put my two cents in.

"Well, he's been saying that he was knocked unconscious and placed in the cage when the 'bad guys'— his words, not mine—broke their bear/partner out."

"But that doesn't explain anything," Dad burst out. "It doesn't explain how he knows about all of this! Or where his brother is! Or anything!"

I thought of Micah, still imprisoned in the body of a feathered cougar and smiled. That had certainly raised some eyebrows.

"What he's saying makes very little sense, if you look at it logically. And he has to be very careful about how much he tells, because he's still going with the 'mistaken identity' plea."

Dad snorted. "Actually, the truth doesn't make much sense, if you're trying to look at it logically."

I smiled. Two men who turned themselves into animals so that they could rob banks? Dad was right. It didn't sound logical.

Amy shrugged. "Anyway, he's getting plenty of mileage with his 'I-wasn't-anywhere-around-and-you-can't-prove-I-was' story."

Dad was quiet. "So what you're saying is that Roddy, whom they arrested as the 'animal trainer' whose animals were robbing banks, is now claiming that he had nothing to do with it, but that the robberies were all committed by people who had turned themselves into animals."

"Umm . . . yes."

"And there are people actually listening to this? Taking it seriously?"

"Well there are people listening. I'm not so sure about the 'taking seriously' part."

Dad laughed. "Okay, I'm not as concerned, now."

Amy smiled. "I just thought you'd want to know."

"Thank you. I do."

"Also, there's been some US army guy hanging around town the past couple of days. Asking questions about you. Where you live. What your studies are. That sort of thing."

Dad looked at me, then back at Amy. "General Dune?"

"Yes. I think that was his name."

"We've met. Just this afternoon." Dad grinned. "Just before you got here, in fact."

"Was that the military-looking vehicle that narrowly missed me as I pulled in?"

Dad shrugged. "Must have been. There aren't that many military vehicles around here." He laughed. "I almost didn't let you in when you knocked. I thought it was our dear General returning."

"The general was out here, trying to get Dad to join the army, or something like that," I put in.

Dad half-smiled. "Yeah. Join the army."

"Really? That's all? Because he sure has been interested in you."

"Well, I'm an interesting guy," Dad said lightly.

Amy looked at him.

"He wants to take me to a military installation and give me a lab there. Work on improving the Essence. Make it last longer."

Amy caught her breath. "You're not seriously considering it, are you, Hank? Because you know that once the military get hold of it . . ."

Dad shook his head. "I told him I wasn't interested." He smiled. "In fact, I've decided to turn it over to our military. They can use it in their peace-keeping efforts."

"Well that's a relief."

Dad smiled and squeezed my shoulder. "My most important work is here, being a dad to Todd."

Amy smiled as well. "And I'd say that's pretty important."

"I kind of like it," I put in.

"So any other choice bits of gossip from the town mills?"

"No, that's about it," she laughed. "Except that a lot of people have been asking about . . ." her eyes widened and she turned a bright red.

Dad laughed. "About us?"

Amy shook her head and covered her face with her hands. "I can't believe I just blurted that out!" Her words were slightly muffled.

Dad reached for one of her hands. "If they ask again, you can tell them that Hank is very, very interested," he said softly.

"Not just very?"

"Very. Very."

Amy smiled.

I left.

Chapter Five

"Hey, Iverson! What's you dad cooking up in his lab, eh?"

Laughter.

I stared at the back of the kid who had spoken as I stepped off the bus.

Rich, Jami and JoJo were waiting for me.

"What the heck was that about?"

Rich shrugged. "Oh, some stupid story about your dad being the next Dr. Moreau."

"Who?"

"Exactly." Rich grinned.

"It's a story about a man who turns animals human . . . or maybe it's the other way around," Jami said. "Anyway, he has this island and the animal/humans are his servants and some of them, or all of them go crazy. Including the good doctor."

"It was made into a movie a couple of times," JoJo put in. "One of them starred Marlon Brando." She smiled. "We should watch it!"

I shuddered. "No, a little too close to home," I said quietly.

JoJo laughed. "Chalk to cheese," she said.

Rich looked at her. "Jo, sometimes I don't understand a thing you say!"

JoJo stuck her tongue out at him. "I mean that comparing your dad's work to Dr. Moreau is like comparing chalk to cheese. Two totally different things."

"Oh."

She shook her head. "Sometimes I wonder why I hang out with you guys!"

I felt a pang. I didn't know why she hung out with us, either. My greatest fear was that one day she would look in

47

a mirror, notice how beautiful she was, then look at me and say to herself, "Why?"

She threw her arms around me and gave me a hug. "I didn't mean it, T," she laughed. "I couldn't survive without you!"

I smiled, weakly. Right. Sure.

"Let's go. First period is about to start."

Jami headed to her class and the three of us hurried to math.

Mrs. Jefferies stared at us over her glasses. "Almost late. Again."

"Sorry, Ma'am," Rich said, moving closer to her desk. "Just got busy . . . talking . . . and didn't notice the time."

Her expression softened as she looked at Rich.

"Well, that's fine, Mr. Walters. Please take your seats."

"Teachers pet!" JoJo whispered, bumping Rich with her elbow.

"At least we know why JoJo keeps *you* around!" I added.

"Come to order, class!"

I sighed. My brain and I had never been very good friends, and it was never more obvious than in math class.

I opened my book.

* * *

"So, Iverson, what's the deal with your dad?"

I looked up at the student who had spoken and swallowed my partially-chewed bite of peanut butter sandwich.

"Nothing, Barry, why do you ask?"

He leaned against the table. "Well everyone's talking about how your dad's experimenting with animals. Creating some sort of potion that can cause them to change into humans."

I snorted.

"There's even been some talk about what he's done to you."

I almost choked on my next bite. "Me?"

"Yeah. Like whether you're really his son. Or even human."

JoJo smiled. "Well, sometimes when I look at him, I wonder myself."

"Thanks Jo. You've made my day."

She laughed and made a face at me.

Barry shrugged. "Well, I just thought that you should hear what's being said."

"So, Barry, tell me, did you believe it?" JoJo asked, one eyebrow raised.

"Well, it does sound kind of far-fetched."

"*Kind* of far-fetched?"

"Well . . . stupid, really."

"Exactly." She took a drink of her juice box. "You can tell them from me that Todd is everything he appears to be. Nothing more. Nothing less."

Red-headed. Freckled. Tall, though not as clumsy as he once was. Definitely not from the deep end of the gene pool. Yep, that's Todd. And thank you, JoJo, for pointing it out. I sighed and looked at the vision sitting next to me, eating nachos from a bag.

JoJo smiled, put an arm around my shoulders, and gave me a kiss on the cheek.

My whole face blossomed crimson.

Rich and Jami laughed from the other side of me. "See what we have to put up with, Barry?" Rich asked. "These two are disgusting!"

Barry watched us for a moment. Then he turned and walked away.

I looked at JoJo.

"You kissed me!"

"I know."

"Not that I'm complaining, because I'm certainly not but . . . ummm . . . why?"

"Because you're just so cute!"

"Oookay . . . What's the real reason?"

She laughed. "T, you're the best. I just love you!" She got to her feet and picked up her bag. "See you in class!" She disappeared into the crowd near the doorway.

Leaving me frozen in my chair, one hand lifted to my cheek.

"Hey, Iverson!"

I could still feel those soft lips, pressed against it.

"Earth to Iverson!"

I'll never wash that cheek again.

"C'mon, buddy, we've got to get to class!" Rich levered me to my feet and steered me into Chemistry.

JoJo was already there.

My mouth stretched into a foolish grin.

"Oh, man, have you got it bad!" Rich muttered into my ear.

My grin stretched wider as I stared at her.

JoJo laughed. "Sit down, Todd, you look like a goof ball!"

Pretty normal for me, Jo. You mean you've just noticed? I fell into my chair.

JoJo laughed again.

By the end of class, I was pretty much back to normal, even though I could feel my face redden every time I looked at Jo . . .

"Geeze, Todd, quit staring at JoJo!"

. . . which was fairly often.

Finally, the four of us were standing out at the bus stop.

"Oh, here's your bus, T!" JoJo waved at the driver, Orman.

Orman waved back, smiling foolishly.

I stared at him. Did I look like that?

"Yes, you look exactly like that!" Rich said into my ear.

I groaned.

"Call me later!" JoJo gave me a push toward the bus.

Numbly, I climbed the steps and dropped into the first available seat. I glanced out the window.

JoJo waved to me, then walked away.

Rich and Jami moved off in the opposite direction.

* * *

"So are you going to tell me about it?" Dad asked.

"Huh? What?"

He smiled. "Well, you've hardly tasted anything you've eaten . . ."

I looked down at my empty plate. I had eaten?

"And you keep sighing."

I took a deep breath, then rolled my eyes and grinned at him.

"JoJo?"

"Who else?"

He laughed. "So what's so different about this day?"

"She . . . she kissed me."

"Really? Did you kiss her back?"

"Well . . . no. There wasn't time."

"Oh, so you need time?"

"Well, you see, she kissed me on the cheek, then got up and went to class."

"And you didn't run after her, tackle her and kiss her back?"

"Dad!"

51

He laughed again. "You are so my boy."

"I am?"

"But at least you're getting started earlier. In grade nine. Not in your first year of college, like me."

"You mean you didn't get your first kiss . . .?"

"Until I was in college. Yes." Dad smiled. "I'm not particularly proud of it, son, but the truth of the matter is that I was so interested in *science* that I really didn't have time for *biology*."

I stared at him. "But isn't biology a sci . . . oh, I get it."

His smile widened. "Yep. Once I met your mother everything changed. She, uh, she chased me until I caught her."

"Ah. So I'm not so weird after all."

Dad laughed. "Oh, I wouldn't go that far!"

"Dad!"

"So she kissed you, did she?"

"Right in front of everyone."

Dad raised his eyebrows. "Significant."

"Really?"

"Yeah. Like laying a claim."

I was silent. JoJo had laid claim? To me?

I was back in my happy place.

Dad reached for the day's paper, sitting in the middle of the table, unopened. He spread it wide.

"Oh, my word!"

"What is it, dad?"

"Ms. Scott!"

I sighed. "Who is she bothering now?"

"No one. Ever again."

"What?"

"According to this headline, she's dead!"

Chapter Six

I leaned over him. "You're kidding me!"

"I wish I were!" Dad pointed to the headline. 'Woman's Body Recovered From River'. There was a large picture of several emergency crew members lifting a wrapped bundle into the back of a waiting ambulance.

"You're sure it's the same Ms. Scott?"

Dad looked at me, disgusted, then pointed to a smaller picture, inserted at the bottom of the article.

The red hair. The cat-like eyes.

He was right. There could only be one Ms. Scott.

I sat down and leaned over the paper. "So what happened?"

"Just a moment. I'm reading."

I fidgeted impatiently as I waited.

Finally, Dad sat back.

"So?"

"Well, they're not really sure. She was seen, walking along the river with a man. Witnesses say they saw the man get into a car a short time later, but that they didn't see her with him."

"Then, a while later, an elderly man was walking his dogs in the same area and one of the dogs spotted the body, floating face down near the shore."

"So her companion must have pushed her in."

"Well, that's one possibility. I'm fairly certain that the police are hot after the guy who was with her. For questioning, if nothing else."

"But it must have been him!"

"Son, they're not even sure it was murder yet. She might have slipped and fallen in on her own. Maybe had a dizzy spell . . ."

"Oh. Right."

"Hard to believe, though." Dad put his chin in his hands and continued to look at the article.

"Yeah. She was just here a couple of days ago. Annoying us."

Dad half-smiled. "Strange, isn't it, that the moment someone dies, you immediately regret anything you said that might have offended them?"

"Yeah. I guess we want them to take good reports to the other side."

Dad stared at me for a moment, then burst out laughing. "Exactly, Son!"

"Well, I am sorry that she's dead," I said, getting up and starting to gather the dishes. "It's sad when anyone dies young. And she was still fairly young."

"It is, and she was." Dad continued to study the article.

I quickly loaded the dishwasher and went to start my homework.

Dad was still staring at the newspaper when I went in to say good night.

* * *

The school was abuzz with the news of the death the next morning.

Sad as I was for Ms. Scott, I was relieved that her news had managed to push my dad and me off everyone's front page.

"So was she murdered?"

I was walking past a group of seniors clustered in the hall.

"Not sure yet. Evidence is inconclusive. No bruising. No sign of a struggle."

"But she could have been pushed?"

"Well, that is one theory. But by whom. And why?"

"So no motive."

"Trust me. That's exactly what they are trying to find right now."

She had been really, really annoying. Could that be a motive? I slapped myself mentally. Come on, Todd. She wasn't that bad. She had actually been rather nice to Dad and me. She had even kept our story out of the . . . Now there's a thought!

I couldn't wait to get home.

"Dad, do you suppose Ms. Scott's death had anything to do with us?"

Dad looked up at me and sighed. "I was afraid you would put that together, Todd. And I think it might."

"That's a little scary."

"A little more than a little."

I blinked. "What?"

"Well, I've been thinking about it today, son, and this is what I've come up with so far. Miranda knew about the Essence. She told her boss."

"Okay."

"Then he cooked up a scheme to sell the Essence to the military."

"So what does that prove?"

"Well, this is where I start to speculate." Dad rubbed his ear.

"Go ahead."

"Then he told someone in the military."

"At least one person in the military."

"Exactly." Dad took a deep breath. "Anyway, the military shows interest. The military has money. Suddenly the Essence is worth something. A substantial something if the military is involved."

I was getting the hang of this. "Her boss suddenly sees a chance of making big money. All he has to do is sit on the story and negotiate with the military!"

"Ms. Scott objects."

"Threatens to expose him."

Dad nodded. "Covers all of the bases."

"Pretty clever."

"Now, none of it could be true," he said. "She might have simply slipped and hit her head. Purely an accident."

We looked at each other.

I shook my head. "It doesn't feel right, Dad."

"For me, either."

"So. Murder for money."

"Yeah. Something new and different."

* * *

Ms. Scott's death was the main topic of conversation for several days.

But when no new evidence was turned up and nothing was offered by the police, people started finding other things to occupy them.

"Iverson! Your dad make you any new friends lately?" Laughter.

I sighed, suddenly wishing for another murder.

"Iverson, I think I just saw your brother! He was rolling in something smelly out in the ditch!" More laughter.

JoJo hugged me. "Don't pay any attention, T," she said. "If you don't react, they'll give it up as a lost cause."

"They're the lost cause," Rich muttered.

"I can't believe you used to hang out with them," JoJo said, turning to Rich.

"Don't remind me! Anyway, that was before . . ."

"Before what?"

He grinned at her. "Before I found out what true friendship was."

I was surprised. Sometimes Rich seemed like a brainless jock. At others, he showed surprising depth.

Later, I leaned back in my bus seat and sighed. In spite of the occasional catcall, it had been a pretty good day. Fairly easy math test first period. New novel assignment in English. Soggy peanut butter for lunch. Laughing with Jo and Rich when Jim's experiment blew up in chemistry. And teasing Rich and Jami at a pep-rally last period instead of going to Social.

Yep. All-in-all, a good day.

I rested my head against the window, feeling the bus rumble over the gravel roads.

I waved half-heartedly at Barry as he got up to leave. I glanced around at the empty seats. Because I lived the furthest from town, I was the last to be dropped off. I didn't mind. It was time when I could just sit and think. When nothing and no one intruded.

"Hey!"

I looked at the bus driver, Orman. He was staring through the windshield at something.

I, too looked through the spotted glass.

Two black SUV's, parked side-by-side, were almost completely blocking the road.

"What are those idiots doing? Can't they talk somewhere else?"

Orman stepped on the brake.

Several doors in the vehicles opened and figures, all dressed entirely in black, began to emerge.

Huh. Not something you saw often.

Or ever, here on the back roads near Milk River.

"I don't like the look of this," Orman said. "Hang on, Iverson!"

He suddenly stepped on the gas and swerved, letting the left wheels slide off the shoulder and down into the ditch.

The men dove back inside their vehicles.

I could vaguely hear them shouting.

Orman pulled the clumsy bus back onto the road, narrowly missing the outside truck.

I looked back as we sped down the road. Their lights had come on. They were going to come after us!

I moved into the seat directly behind the driver. "Um, Orman, I think they're going to follow."

He glanced in the mirror. "They can try," he said, grinning. He floored the gas pedal.

Just then, directly ahead, a cattle liner came over a rise toward us. The driver saw us immediately, slowed and pulled over to the right on the narrow road.

Orman sighed and did the same.

The liner driver waved as we edged past each other.

Orman gave him a cheerful salute, then looked ahead. We were at the top of a hill and could see quite a distance. Four more of the huge trucks were coming toward us, spaced out over a half-mile.

"I guess the Jones' are shipping their calves this week," I said, unnecessarily.

"Looks like it," Orman agreed. He glanced back in his mirror and nodded.

I twisted around.

The two SUV's had edged out onto an approach and were just sitting there. Then, as I watched, they pulled in behind the first liner and started back toward town.

"Well, I guess that's that," Orman said.

"That was weird."

"For a minute, I felt like James Bond," Orman grinned.

Yeah. James Bond driving a clumsy yellow school bus. I smiled. Not a picture that came easily.

* * *

"D'you think they were really after us?"

Dad was staring at me, his fork suspended over his plate.

"I . . . really couldn't say, son," he managed at last.

"Well, it seemed really odd, the way they were parked, first of all."

"Well, you know city folks, son. They don't have a handle on country etiquette."

"Yeah, but to block almost the entire road?"

"Well, they probably didn't realize that it is as busy as it is."

I stared at him. "Really, Dad?" I could hear the scepticism in my own voice.

Dad colored slightly.

"And then to get out of the vehicle just as Orman and I pulled up."

"Have you thought that maybe they needed help?"

"Nope. Didn't think that for a minute," I said. "Fancy cars. Fancy clothes. Those guys had 'On Star' or at least their own cell phones. They didn't need our help."

Dad was silent. He finally took a bite of pie and chewed slowly.

"So what are you thinking?" I asked him.

He shook his head. "I don't know what to think, Todd," he said. "It does sound rather . . . strange."

"Strange doesn't even begin to describe it."

* * *

"I'm sure you're right," JoJo said.

"I agree," Rich added.

I sighed. "So why would they be after me?"

"Well, you remember what the General said? About you and your dad being in danger?"

59

"Only if the word got out . . ."

JoJo looked at me. "Todd, I think we can safely assume that the word has gotten out."

"So what are you guys discussing so seriously?" Jami had come up behind us.

"Oh! James!" Rich smiled and put an arm around her shoulders. "Didn't hear you."

"I'll try to stomp louder," Jami said, smiling back. "So what are we discussing?"

"Well, Todd had a strange experience last night on his way home from school," JoJo said.

"Yeah. A couple of SUV's full of black-clad spies tried to hold him up." Rich's smile stretched into a grin.

"You're kidding!"

"Actually, he's not," I said. "They were blocking the road somewhere between Sproad's corner and the ranch. I don't know what would have happened, because lead-foot Orman managed to squeeze past them and get away. But it sure looked suspicious."

Jami stared at me. "That doesn't sound good, Todd," she said, seriously.

JoJo nodded. "I agree."

"Well, anyway, I told my dad and he's going to look into it."

"But they might be after the . . ." she leaned forward, ". . . Essence." The last was whispered.

"Actually, that's what we think as well," Rich said.

"Everyone will be after it."

I nodded, unhappily.

"So what can we do?" As usual, JoJo wanted to be prepared.

"Well, I think we should keep an eye on Todd, at the very least," Jami suggested.

"Yeah, because we'd be such good protection," Rich said, shaking his head.

"Well, who knows? Maybe if he's always surrounded by people, nobody will try anything," Jami said.

I frowned. I suddenly felt . . . important.

It was a new thing for me.

"Okay, that takes care of school," JoJo said. "What about the drive to and from?"

I shrugged. "I don't know what can be done, there."

"Yeah, he was with Orman when . . ."

"Big, threatening Orman," Rich laughed.

"Well, what do we do?" JoJo demanded. "Hire a body-guard?"

"Well, I think we should call the police," Jami said.

"And tell them what?" JoJo looked at her.

"Well, that there were some suspicious vehicles on the road, at least."

I nodded. "Yeah, we could tell them that without giving away any specifics."

"They are always on the lookout for smugglers," Rich said. "And they would patrol the road more."

"Okay. So . . . school. Who wants the first shift?"

I rolled my eyes. Okay, so . . . feelings of importance? Gone. Feelings of being four years old again? Just starting.

* * *

"Hey, Walters! The coach wants to talk to you!"

Rich sighed. "I'll be right back, T," he said. "Who knows what he wants!"

He disappeared through the dressing room doorway.

I finished tying my shoes. Then I stood up and turned to stow my gear back in my locker.

* * *

"Geeze, they didn't waste any time!"

I opened my eyes and squinted against the glare.

Rich and JoJo were staring down at me.

"Who are 'they', Mr. Walters?"

Oh, man, that sounded like . . . I turned my head. The basketball coach was standing on the other side of me.

Rich rolled his eyes and rubbed a hand over his face.

"Todd? Todd are you all right?" JoJo asked.

I looked toward her. "Fine, I think," I said. I winced and rubbed a tender spot on the back of my head. "What happened?"

Coach cleared his throat. "You must have slipped on the wet floor, Todd."

"And . . . ummm . . . hit your head," Rich added with a sidelong glance at Coach.

Oh. Great.

I sat up. So far, so good. Rich and JoJo helped me stand, then led me over to the bench.

"How are you feeling, Todd?" Coach had followed us.

"Okay, I guess," I said. I rubbed my hand over that sore spot again.

"That's where you must have hit your head," he said. He touched the spot with gentle fingers. "You've got quite a lump. Maybe we should call for the ambulance."

"No, I'm all right," I said. "I just want to sit here for a moment."

Coach eyed me doubtfully. "Are you sure?"

"I'm sure. I don't even have a headache."

"Sight okay?"

"Yeah. No blurred vision or anything."

"Well, all right. But if you start feeling . . . nauseous or anything, you let someone know immediately."

"I will."

He looked at me one last time, then shrugged and left the room.

"So what happened?"

"Hey! Why is there a girl in the boy's dressing room?"

A couple of boys, wrapped in towels came out of the showers.

"Don't worry, I'm leaving!" JoJo said. She stood up. "Can you walk, T?"

"Of course I can walk!" I stood up. "I'm fine. See?" I wavered slightly and JoJo clutched my arm.

"Hey! No girls allowed!" Another boy was frantically wrapping himself in his towel.

"Let's get out of here!" she muttered.

She and Rich led me to the cafeteria and sat me in a chair. JoJo slid onto the table in front of me and leaned forward. "So what happened?"

I rubbed my head again. "I must have slipped."

Rich snorted. "No."

I looked at him.

"Don't you remember?"

"I remember Rich leaving to talk to the coach and me tying my shoes and turning to put my stuff away." I frowned. Had there been voices? Oh, great, Todd, now you're hearing voices.

"Well, the coach hadn't sent for me," Rich said. "That was just a trick to get me out of the room."

"What?!"

"Yeah. I met Coach just outside the door and he was definitely not thinking about me." Rich smiled. "In fact, I don't think he was thinking about basketball at all. He was talking to his wife. Or rather, kissing his wife." Rich wiggled his eyebrows.

JoJo laughed.

"So then?"

63

"I went right back into the room. And there were these two guys standing over you."

"Guys?"

"Yeah. Dressed in shorts and Eagles shirts, but not anyone I recognized."

"So what were they doing?"

"Well, one of them was crouched down beside you when I came in, but as soon as they saw me, they took off."

"So Todd might have just fallen and hit his head?" JoJo said.

"I don't think so," Rich said. "Those two guys looked really suspicious to me." He shrugged. "Anyway, I hollered and the coach came running in."

"And me," JoJo said. "I was waiting just down the hall."

"Well, I don't know about you guys, but these things are adding up to a bit more than coincidence," I said.

"You're so right, T," JoJo said.

"We've got to call the police," Rich said.

"I'm going to talk to my dad tonight."

* * *

"So where is he?" JoJo sounded worried.

"I don't know, Jo. He's not answering the home phone or his cell."

JoJo frowned. "I don't like this."

"Neither do I, but what can I do?"

The two of us were standing at the bus stop. My bus, and Orman, were waiting beside us.

"Well, your dad told you to wait for him to drive you home."

"Yeah, but he was going to be here right at 3." I glanced at my watch. "It's 3:25."

"Iverson, are you coming?" Orman was starting to sound impatient. "There are other kids on the bus besides you!"

"Sorry, Orman, I just don't know what to do!"

"Ummm . . . get on the bus?"

I rolled my eyes, sighed and nodded. "Well, I guess I'll ride the bus," I told JoJo.

She clutched my arm. "I don't know, T. I have a bad feeling about this."

"Well, I think it would be worse for me to stay here at the school by myself."

JoJo looked around. The grounds were deserted, except for us.

"You could come to my house."

"But you said that there's no one there, either."

"Well, I'd be there."

I looked at her. Tall, slender, figure. Long silky hair. Nope. Not someone I'd hide behind during a brawl.

"No, Jo, I'll just head home. There are more border patrols now and anyway, they'd be stupid to try the same thing twice."

"They're not stupid, T."

"Right." I climbed the steps into the bus. "See you . . ."

The door closed with a snap, cutting off the rest of my sentence. Orman stepped on the gas.

I dropped into the first available seat and looked out the window as JoJo slid past.

She looked worried.

That made two of us.

The bus ride seemed interminable. One by one, Orman let the kids off at their stops. Finally, a century later, I was once again the last passenger.

I leaned my head back against the bus seat and sighed.

"Hey, Iverson! You awake?

I looked forward.

Orman was watching me in the rear-view mirror.

"Yeah?" Please, please, please don't bring up our wild bus trip again. I don't think I could bear rehashing it one more time.

"Just wondering if you'd heard the story that your friend Rich's Uncle Roddy was telling?"

Relief. "Yeah, I've heard it."

"I wondered, because he's starting to point fingers. And one of the fingers he's pointing is at your dad."

I sat up. "My dad?"

"Yeah. He's saying that your dad might have had something to do with the robberies Roddy's accused of."

"What?!"

"I know. Weird, huh?"

"So does anyone believe him?"

"Well, you know how people love to talk."

"Boy do I ever!" I said under my breath.

"Well, there's some who are wishing they could talk to your dad about what he does in that lab of his way out in the country."

I rolled my eyes. "Well, you can tell them from me that all he does is try to find better ways of feeding animals."

"Oh, something like animal nutrition."

"Yes, something like animal . . ."

I got no further.

The bus suddenly . . . dropped.

And I was flung through the air.

Chapter Seven

I smelled . . . Pinesol.

Weird.

Mom had loved it. She had used it when house-breaking her dogs. But Dad had given it up when I was little because it always reminded him of puppy pee.

I opened one eye. Huh. Shivering grey walls. Cinder block. I opened the other eye. More of the same.

Definitely not my bedroom, unless Dad had done some radical remodelling while I was asleep.

Asleep? Why had I been asleep?

And where was I?

I tried to turn my head. Okay. Note to self. Never, ever try to turn my head.

The pain blossomed from somewhere behind my left ear. I closed my eyes again.

Better.

Much, much later I again pried one eye open. Same grey walls. But this time, they weren't shivering. This time, they stayed put.

Like walls are supposed to do.

I moved my eye as far as I could without making the mistake of moving my head. More grey walls. And part of a wardrobe. I assumed that the rest of the wardrobe was there as well, but I wasn't going to risk movement to confirm.

I moved my eye in the opposite direction. More walls. Huh. I was surrounded by them.

No windows, though, that I could see.

A small table was immediately beside me, complete with a dimly lighted lamp. From the near-darkness in the room, I assumed that this small lamp was my only illumination.

I heard the sound of a door. Then a blinding light. I gasped and closed my eye.

Someone paused in the doorway.

"Still sleeping?"

"Let's hope he's just sleeping, Egleson."

"I'm sorry, sir. I did the best I could!"

"Best? We almost lost him!"

Him? Were they discussing me?

"In my defence, sir," Egleson said, "everything looked entirely natural."

"Sure. Natural. Yet, somehow you missed a pothole the size of Kansas?"

"Their camouflage was impeccable. Almost perfect."

There was a pause. Then, "So what you're telling me is that, without anyone noticing, they managed to dig a hole big enough for a bus to fall into, cover the hole perfectly, and then somehow lay hidden on the bald prairie to scoop up their prize?"

Hmm. Now I was a prize?

"Pretty much the whole story, sir," Egleson said.

'Sir' snorted sceptically.

"We did manage to intervene in time to pick up the boy," Egleson went on.

Boy. Yep. Me, again.

"But lost the guys who set the trap!"

"Well, we were trying to determine if the boy had been injured . . ." Egleson said.

'Sir' was obviously out of patience. "Go on. Get out of here! We'll discuss this later!"

Shuffling footsteps retreated.

Then someone came into the room, walking heavily. "Here, Lieutenant."

Another person entered. This one, quite a bit lighter on their feet. I could hardly hear the footsteps and almost jumped when a woman's voice spoke immediately beside me.

"He looks all right to me, General." Gentle fingers touched my forehead and turned my head slightly toward the light.

Oh, please don't turn . . . ouch.

"He's got a nasty bruise here on the side of his head and that will probably give him some grief when he wakes up."

I felt a draft on bare flesh. I gasped and opened both eyes.

Through the blossoming pain, I saw a young woman in army fatigues standing beside the bed, a rough, green blanket clutched in her hands. Another shadowy figure stood just out of my line of sight. And I was lying there, naked, in front of both of them.

"Ah. Awake, I see." The second figure had spoken.

Instinctively, I tried to turn my head. Oh. Right. No head-turning. I groaned aloud.

"Sorry, son, but I'm afraid you will have a nasty headache for a while." The second person stayed just out of my sight. The voice sounded familiar, but I simply couldn't place it.

"Yes," the woman agreed. She spread the blanket over me once more. "You've had a nasty accident, Todd, and it will take some time for you to recover."

I moved my hands under the blanket. Then my feet. Relief. Everything seemed to be present and accounted for.

"A-accident?" My voice came out gravelly and thin.

"Yes, Todd. Don't you remember?" The woman's voice was calm. Soothing.

I puckered up my face. The last thing I remembered was talking to Orman on the bus. He had said something about my dad. That was all I could remember.

"I . . . ummm . . . remember being on the bus," I said hesitantly.

"Yes, and there was an accident."

Huh. Maybe that was why I didn't remember getting off at my stop.

I hadn't.

The second person spoke again. "The bus hit a hole in the road and, because the driver wasn't paying attention, he lost control and hit the ditch."

"Is . . . is Orman okay?"

"He's a bit bruised and has a broken arm, but, yes, he'll be okay."

"Oh. Ummm . . . good." For some reason, I felt the prickle of tears. What on earth was wrong with me? I didn't even like Orman!

"Now, the lieutenant is going to look after you." The second person moved and I heard the squeak of a door. "I'll be in my office if you have any concerns, Lieutenant." The door closed.

"Well, let's have a look at you, shall we?" The woman ran gentle fingers across my aching head and down my neck. She lifted my head slightly and turned it back and forth, keeping her fingers along my spine. Then she lowered my head and again reached for the blanket.

This time, I was a bit more prepared. I grabbed the edge of it.

"I just need to give you a quick check-up, Todd," she said.

I hung on grimly.

"I have to know that there isn't anything we've overlooked."

"I can give you a pretty good assessment," I said. "My head hurts like crazy, especially when I try to move it. Other than that, everything else seems to be in good working order."

"Well, that's good to hear, but I really should check for myself."

I just stared at her and hung on to my blanket.

Finally, she let go and stepped back. "Fine," she said. "But if you feel pain, would you please call me?"

"You mean besides my head?"

She smiled. "Yes, besides your head."

"Ummm . . . sure."

"I'll leave you, then." She disappeared from my sight. I heard the door open and close.

I sighed and closed my eyes again.

* * *

Bathroom. Corner. Locked door. Tray shelf. Wall. Corner. Wall. Bed. Table. More wall. Corner.

I had been in this room for two days, judging by the regular appearance of trays of food. Feeling a bit better, I had managed to get out of bed and was making my slow way around the room, taking inventory; blanket clutched to my naked body.

Wardrobe. Wall. Corner. And I was back at the bathroom.

What was this place? How did I get here?

And, more importantly, why?

I moved to the wardrobe and pulled one of the doors open.

Clothes. Neatly folded.

I pulled out the top garment. A T-shirt. Just about my size.

I didn't hesitate. I dropped my blanket and pulled the shirt over my head. Then I rummaged until I managed to find a pair of sweat pants. They were a bit big, but more stylish and certainly more convenient than my blanket. I stepped into them and tied them into place.

Then I threw my blanket on the bed.

I opened one of the wardrobe drawers. Huh. Socks. And underwear.

I glanced at the door, which had remained closed since someone had come in to take my used tray. Then I quickly slid my pants off, put on a clean pair of underwear and re-donned the pants.

Carrying a pair of socks, I sat on the bed to pull them on.

I went to the bathroom mirror to see how I looked.

I shook my head and grinned. "Stylin', Todd," I told myself. But at least I was covered and didn't feel quite so vulnerable.

There was a sudden knock at the door. I jumped. "Umm . . . come in?" Why was I even saying it? The first thing I had learned about this room was that the door was securely locked. From the outside.

Whoever was out there could certainly come and go as they wished.

The door opened. The young lieutenant stepped inside, carrying the inevitable tray, which she set on my bed.

"Oh, good, you're up," she said. She put her hands on her hips and looked at me. "And you've found your clothes. Double-good."

"Yeah. Hooray for me."

She smiled. "How are you feeling?"

"Well, physically, apart from a slight headache, okay, if I keep my movements small. Mentally, not so good."

"What can I help you with?"

"Well, for one, you can explain to me where I am. And why."

She shook her head. "I'm afraid I can't tell you very much."

"Can you at least tell me why I am a prisoner here?"

She hesitated. Finally, "You're not really a prisoner, Todd."

"But the locked door would suggest otherwise."

She half-smiled. "Yes, I suppose it would."

"So?"

"You are in a government installation. You have been brought here for your own protection."

"Someone is going to try to hurt me?"

"Well . . . yes."

"Where is my dad? Does he know I'm here?"

"Yes, he does."

"And?"

"And what?" She looked puzzled.

"Where is he?"

"He's . . . in the lab."

"There's a lab? Here?"

"Ummm . . . yes. And he's in it."

"When can I see him?"

"Well that's the thing." She hesitated again. "You see, he's in a top-secret part of the compound and you are in the . . . protected part. They really don't . . . connect."

"So what you are telling me is that I am locked up in the dungeon and that my dad is being held in the room reserved for mad scientists."

The Lieutenant half-smiled.

"Aren't you?"

"No, Todd. You are being kept here for your own protection."

"Right. So, what's for dinner?"

"I've left you your tray. Please eat it all and then set the tray beside your door."

The Lieutenant paused beside the door as though she would say something more. Then she shook her head and left.

I heard the distinct click as she re-locked the door.

I moved over to the tray and sat down beside it. Mmm. Roast beef. Potatoes and gravy. Vegetables. Salad. And a glass of something that looked like grape crush.

Not so bad. If I had to be a captive, at least the food wasn't bad.

I ate every bite.

Finally, I sat back, sipping at the grape drink.

It tasted a bit odd, but somehow familiar, and was sweet and satisfying. I tipped the glass up and swallowed the last of it.

Then I realized why it seemed so familiar. I had tasted it before. Just before I had assumed the shape of an animal.

They were feeding me Essence.

Chapter Eight

There was the usual disorientation. I was suddenly looking way, way up at the ceiling. My eyes were on either side of my head, so I had to swing it back and forth to get a proper perspective.

I twisted to one side.

A long, scaly body protruded from the pile of cloth that had only recently been my clothing.

Great. A snake. My favourite.

Not.

I tried to move forward, searching in vain for something to help propel me. No arms. No legs. No appendages of any sort.

How did one move in this body?

I swung my head to one side. My body . . . flexed. I lifted it, dragging my tail forward. Then I pressed my stomach to the ground and let my front end slide forward. This worked . . . sort of.

The scales on my belly seemed to flex a bit as I moved and I realized that they were actually gripping the surface beneath me.

For several minutes, I practiced the 'inchworm' method of movement, praying the whole time that I wouldn't have to get anywhere quickly.

I had managed to make my way nearly to the door when it opened. Suddenly.

"Oh, look at you!" A large figure knelt down beside me.

Quick! Hide! I curled myself into a ball. Clever, Todd.

I stuck my tongue out at him. Huh. The air . . . tasted.

No. He tasted. I stuck my tongue out again.

Flick.

Flick.

I could smell pancakes. And sausages. With maple syrup.

Weird.

He reached down and scooped me up into his hands.

I could feel my heart hammering through my long, narrow body.

But he was surprisingly gentle.

"Todd?"

I lifted my head and looked at him.

Flick.

Suddenly, I knew why the second person in the room had seemed familiar.

An oddly elongated General Dune was holding me in his two pudgy hands.

"This is astounding!" he muttered. "I never would have believed it!" He set me down on top of my discarded clothing.

I struggled to put some distance between us, but he watched me closely, following my every movement.

"I see. I see," he muttered to himself. "Yes. It takes a while to get used to the new body. That's something we will have to allow for. Training. Training." He stood there, watching me and nodding.

The whole scenario seemed suddenly . . . grotesque. Like a scene out of a 'B' grade horror flick.

I had made it almost to the bathroom when the general reached out and scooped me up again. He set me back on my pile of clothes.

Sigh.

Once more, I started toward the bathroom.

Again, he watched. Again, he moved me back when I nearly reached my goal.

This was rapidly getting old.

Finally, he picked me up and carried me over to the table lamp. There, he closely examined my face and body.

I turned my head and tried a new tactic. Hissing.

"Perfect! Perfect!"

Yeah. That seemed to be as effective as everything else I had tried.

He set me carefully down on the bed.

"The possibilities!" He went to the door and pulled it open, stepping through. Then he shut it behind him and I heard the lock snap. Footsteps retreated.

This couldn't be good.

I closed my eyes, waiting to feel like myself again.

* * *

"Todd?"

I turned my head.

"That is so freaky." The lieutenant set down my supper tray and walked hesitantly across the room toward me.

I looked down at myself.

Oh. Right.

Dog.

I stood up and stretched. Dog-style. Front legs. Then back legs.

I didn't bother to wag my tail. I wasn't feeling particularly friendly.

"I've. . . I've brought you your supper, Todd."

I nodded and jumped up on the bed, nosing the covers off my food. Mmmm. Hamburger. Fries. Salad. And apple pie. Yep. They really did do all right with the food in this prison.

The lieutenant had followed me over to the bed and now she sat down at the end.

I left my exploring and looked at her.

"Is it really you in there?" She reached out a hand.

I curled my lips and she drew back.

"Todd?"

I rolled my eyes and sighed. Then I nodded.

She reached out again. This time, I lowered my head and let her . . . pet me.

She lifted my ear and looked under it. The she touched my lower lip and gently pressed it back, looking at my teeth.

This was so embarrassing.

Finally, she dropped her hand. "This is the most amazing thing I have ever seen!"

I sat down and stared at her.

"Sooo . . . you can think and . . . everything?"

I sighed again and nodded.

"Show me."

After my first few days here, they had brought in a TV and an entertainment system.

Super Mario and Halo, together with an unlimited access to movies, had been keeping me more or less sane.

I jumped off the bed and walked over to my entertainment unit. Pushing the 'on' with my nose, I grabbed the controller with my teeth and carried it back. Then I sat on the floor beside the bed and laid the controller in front of me. Carefully, I tapped the power button with one claw.

The Wii menu blinked into life.

I moved the controller and chose the cross-word icon. Despite the handicap posed by having only paws and a large, wet nose, I was soon following clues and filling in blanks.

The lieutenant shook her head. "I never would have believed it."

I carried the controller back and dropped it on top of the unit. Then I punched the 'off' and returned to the bed.

I looked at the lieutenant, then, pointedly, at my dinner.

"Okay!" She rose from the bed. "I'll leave you to it."

She started toward the door, pausing just after she had it open. "Your father has discovered something that will change lives," she said softly. "I hope he gets a chance to do it."

I stared at the closed door and shrugged.

Okay, where's the salad dressing?

* * *

"Gee, Todd, you're huge!" The lieutenant was staring up at me from the doorway.

Yes. Well. Horses generally are. It's just that we don't usually keep them in our bedrooms.

I swished my tail. Dad had obviously gotten the kinks worked out of the horse Essence.

"This is magnificent. Magnificent!" The General pushed past her. He walked over toward me.

I stamped a hoof and he stopped where he was.

Yeah, that's it, General. Just keep on coming and I'll show you what it means to have flat feet.

He put his hands on his hips. Then he shook his head. "I never would have believed it."

I sighed and sat down on the floor.

No way my chair would hold me. Or my bed.

We stared at each other.

"Well, I've seen enough," the General looked at his watch. "When did he receive the Essence?"

"Oh, it was with his breakfast, so I would say . . . about 4 hours ago."

"We're making good progress," the General said.

Huh. Four hours? How did Dad get it to last so long?

"I'll see you around, Todd," the general spoke from the door.

Yeah. Well. I'll be here.

Chapter Nine

Mario was on his last life. I dodged and leaped and spun. But my efforts were wasted.

The fateful 'death riff' sounded.

Crap.

I threw down the controller in disgust. So close.

I got up off the bed and wandered around the room, stretching and taking deep breaths.

How long had I been here?

Four weeks? Five?

I had lost count.

The food was good, considering almost every meal was served with a liberal helping of Essence. I had turned into more animals than I could count. Cats, both large and small. Dogs. Monkeys. Bears. Gorillas. Snakes. Cows. Horses. Pigs. Birds. Jungle. Desert. Exotic. Domestic.

I think there was even one or two that are imaginary.

But I might have imagined those.

This last one had been a wild pig. And had lasted considerably longer than any of the others.

Dad was definitely succeeding.

They still hadn't allowed me to see or talk to my dad. I was assured he was well and working hard. I would have known that even without their reassurances because I had constant proof of his activities.

I looked down and ran a hand along my arm. It was so nice to feel smooth skin once more. Such a difference from the coarse hair and muscled legs of a wild pig.

Suddenly, Mario didn't interest me. I picked up the controller again and hit the off button then got up and made another circuit of the room.

I was distinctly bored and I missed my dad. And I really, really missed JoJo more than I wanted to admit.

I flung myself back on my cot. What could I possibly do?

After my first few changes, the general had installed cameras in my room, rather than come in and study me himself. I could feel eyes watching me. For that reason, I never was quite comfortable, even in what should have been my own space.

There weren't any cameras in the bathroom, however.

I spent a lot of time in the bathroom.

Every day, even though I was often otherwise occupied with being some animal, I was taken out into a large gymnasium. For a couple of hours, if I was human, I played basketball. If not, I ran and generally moved about a lot. It helped to burn off my pent up steam, but never really made up for my lack of freedom.

Or the presence of someone to talk to.

Though the people I glimpsed in my daily routine seemed kind and sympathetic, none of them spoke to me, other than to give me the day's orders.

I had never really thought of myself as a talker, but this experience had taught me something.

I loved to visit.

I promised myself that if I ever again saw the light of day, I would spend the whole of it talking. To whomever would listen.

I put my hands behind my head and stared up at the featureless ceiling. A long, fluorescent fixture provided ample, even glaring, light. I squinted up at it.

How fun to be out of this box of a room and flying in the open sky. I closed my eyes. I could feel the wind in my breast feathers, coursing through my primaries and tail feathers. I adjusted them slightly, feeling the increase in the power of the wind as I started into my dive.

I opened my eyes. Nothing had changed, except that now I could see two little spiders building intricate webs at either end of the far-off light fixture. I stared at them. Why hadn't I noticed them before?

I turned my head. Everything seemed clearer. Almost like it did when I was an . . . eagle.

I gasped. An eagle! I opened my mouth. "Ahhhh!"

Okay, false alarm. But for a moment, I thought I had begun to change.

But that would be impossible. I hadn't had any Essence since breakfast. When I had turned into a wild pig. I looked again at my arm. My decidedly un-hairy arm.

Too much time to think, Todd, I told myself.

I switched on the TV.

* * *

"So . . . how about a little game of one on one?"
Silence.

"Come on, I promise I won't beat you too badly."
Nothing.

One of my keepers, a private I had nicknamed, 'The Wall', for obvious reasons, had just opened the door to the gym. I stepped past him and switched on the lights.

"Really, I won't tell a soul."

The man stepped back, spun on his heel and closed the door with military precision. The lock clicked.

"Man, what I wouldn't give to have you to forget to lock that thing just once," I muttered under my breath.

I started to run, pumping my arms and revelling in the feeling of freedom. Back and forth across the floor, I ran faster and faster. Finally, completely winded, I leaned back against the wall.

Logically, I knew that I was still in a box. Just a bit larger than my usual one. But emotionally, it felt wonderful to have even this small bit of freedom. And after more than two months, by my reckoning, this was definitely the best part of my day.

I closed my eyes and again, I pictured myself as an eagle.

I could feel the wind. I could feel the sunshine on my back. The cool mist as I sailed through a thick cloud. The sweet, sweet fragrance of pure air.

"Screeech!"

That didn't sound right. I caught my breath and looked down.

My clothes had fallen in a heap around my . . . talons. My head protruded from the collar of a shirt that was suddenly far, far too large. And totally the wrong shape.

I lifted feathered wings and scrambled myself free of the restrictive clothing. Then, without thinking, I leaped into the air. For the moment, I felt nothing but pure joy.

I circled around the ceiling and up and down the room glorying in the delicate shifts in the air, present even in this enclosed space.

Finally, I landed beside my pile of clothes and took a deep breath.

Then the thinking started.

How had this happened? It had been many hours since my last dose of Essence. And that had been a panther. A panther that had lasted for an entire day, or at least breakfast to breakfast. However long that was in this place.

How, then was I able to turn into an eagle? And more importantly, how was I going to turn back? Would it just wear off?

Or was I in deep trouble?

I took another deep breath and calmed myself, then, carefully, deliberately, pictured myself as a human. Smooth skin. Fingers. Toes.

Red hair. Freckles. Okay, I figured I needed to be thorough.

In only seconds, I was featherless and shivering. It had been as easy and painless as taking off a new outfit. Only what an outfit!

I scrambled into my clothes and sat down against the wall. This was getting weirder and weirder.

I was just dozing off when 'The Wall' came to fetch me. He stood back and let me precede him down the hall.

This part of the complex was pretty dull. Long hall, broken at intervals and on either side by heavy doors. Near the end, opposite to my room, was a small alcove with a desk, and equipped with monitors showing various angles of my room. There was usually a man seated at the desk. Another fatigue-clad soldier.

Occasionally, the chair was empty.

"What's the score?" 'The Wall' spoke behind me.

I glanced back at him in surprise. He could talk!

The man behind the desk took an ear bud out of his left ear. "Seven-zip."

"Well, those Raiders better get their butts in gear. I've got 50 bucks riding on that game."

The man behind the desk snickered. "Good luck with that."

"Simmons coming in tomorrow?"

"Well, it is Monday, so he's scheduled, but you know Simmons."

"Party all weekend?"

"Probably."

Two dogs came out from behind the desk. One of them sniffed at me.

'The Wall' tripped over him.

The dog yelped and headed back under the desk.

"Geeze, Gerrold! Can't you keep your dogs under control?"

"Sorry, buddy." The man looked down. "Waldorf, Regency, stay!"

Waldorf? Regency? I suddenly felt sorry for the dogs.

'The Wall' opened my door and ushered me inside.

"Thanks for the . . ." I got no further.

The door was shut and locked.

* * *

I looked for Simmons the next day when my escort arrived to take me to the gym. Sure enough, the desk sat empty. Monitors dark.

So. Mondays. I stored that little bit of information away.

Chapter Ten

The next day, something different was delivered along with my lunch.

General Dune.

Ugh.

He wandered around my room and asked me questions as I ate my meal.

I've had more uncomfortable meals in my lifetime. I think.

No, scratch that.

"So, how are you feeling?"

Ummm . . . besides the fact that I'm a prisoner? "Fine."

"Good. Good." More pacing.

"Are they taking good care of you?"

Well, no one will talk to me and they herd me back and forth like a pet dog. "Yes."

He stopped just inside the door and watched as I forked the last of my lasagne into my mouth. I reached for the glass of juice on the tray.

"Hold it a second, please, Todd."

My hand froze over the glass. I stared at him.

"I need you to come with me."

"Why?" I got to my feet.

"I will tell you when we get there."

I shrugged. "Okay." Did I have a choice? I started to follow him.

"Please bring your drink."

I looked at him and shrugged again. Whatever. I grabbed the glass.

The General led me up the hall toward the gymnasium. I trailed along behind him, clutching my drink.

Finally, he stopped beside one of the doors closest to the gym, then unlocked it and pushed it open. "Come in here," he said, disappearing inside.

I leaned forward suspiciously, peering into the room.

It was a normal little room, with cupboards around three walls and a small hospital cot against the fourth. There was also a glass box standing in the center of the room. A huge, upright glass box with a door standing open in one side.

I stared at it.

"It's all right, Todd, you can go in," the lieutenant had come up soundlessly behind me.

I placed a hand over my heart. "Man, one of these times, you're going to give me a heart attack!"

She smiled. "Sorry, Todd." She nodded toward the room. "Go ahead inside."

I walked in, with her right behind me.

The General had taken up a position on the far side of the room, feet apart and hands clasped behind him. He nodded at the lieutenant, who closed the door behind us.

She crossed over to stand beside him.

Then he looked at me.

"Todd, I want you to take off your clothes and get into the box," he said.

I stared at him. Had I heard him correctly?

"Please."

Was he insane?

"You can leave your underwear on, if you're feeling shy."

Shy? That was the least of what I was feeling right now. I made no move to obey.

"It's not what you think," the lieutenant said.

I looked at her. How could she possibly know what I was thinking?

She sighed. "We are changing you into a very small animal, Todd and we don't want you to get hurt."

Oh, is that all! In that case, I'll jump to obey.

Not.

I stayed where I was.

"Todd, I don't want to have to do this, but if I have to, I will call for help and you will go into the box."

I had heard that tone of voice before. From my dad and the occasional teacher. I sighed, handed my drink to the lieutenant and pulled off my T-shirt.

"The pants, too, Todd."

I stripped them off and dropped them on the floor.

"Now, into the box."

I started toward it slowly.

"Oh, and take your drink."

I held out my hand for the glass and the lieutenant put it into my hand. Then, clutching it, I stepped into the box.

The General shut the door behind me and I heard something slide.

I glanced down. A bolt, fitted into the side of the container. I was locked in.

The box was just tall enough for me to stand comfortably upright. I looked around. The seams looked rather . . . airtight. I put one hand on the glass and stared at my murderers.

This really was a 'B' grade movie.

The General made 'drinking' motions with his hand and I glanced down at the glass in my hand. I had forgotten I was carrying it.

I shrugged and tipped it up, draining it. The familiar taste of Essence hit me immediately.

I set the glass down. When I changed, I didn't want to risk it falling, smashing, and cutting my feet. Or hooves. Or whatever I ended up with.

I felt disoriented. Dizzy. My head was spinning. I leaned against the side of the box and closed my eyes. Slowly, I started to . . . shrink.

I kept my eyes closed. I had discovered that helped.

The air felt different. Alive, somehow. And suddenly, my eyes popped open. I tried to close them.

I couldn't.

I looked around. Everything was . . . separated. Like I was looking through a kaleidoscope. Weird.

I tried to lift my head. It was cumbersome. Difficult.

For several minutes, I simply sat where I was, trying to make sense of my world. Trying to see. Trying to hear. Slowly, I began to feel changes in the air.

Something on my head . . . vibrated. I tipped it to one side. Yes. Changes in the vibrations began to sound like speech. I could 'hear' someone talking. Muffled and strange, but definitely human speech.

I decided to try to move. Two legs closest to my head responded immediately.

So far so good. I was moving forward. Slightly.

Then I discovered two more legs. And beyond them two more.

Great. I was some sort of insect.

I wiggled the second pair of legs. Then the third. Okay, we're doing well. Moving one leg at a time and resting frequently, I struggled forward.

Finally, with a last heave, I managed to escape the pile of cloth that had imprisoned me. I looked around. I realized I was looking at my underwear, magnified dozens of times and fractured into hundreds of little snapshots.

I was suddenly glad that the General had forced me to shed my extra clothes. I had barely managed to conquer Mount Underwear. I never would have made it out of Mount Pantsandshirt.

I crawled away from the cloth and looked around. Or rather, tried to look around.

Nothing looked normal. Everything refused to fuse into one picture. I moved toward the glass wall of my prison.

Huh. At least moving was taking a little less effort. Like trying to walk on your hands and feet and control an extra pair of . . . okay not easy to describe, but getting easier to master.

I reached the wall and put my two front feet on it. They . . . stuck. I tried moving up. The second set stuck. Then the third. I was crawling up the wall.

Cool!

I continued happily, upwards. Then, suddenly, a face loomed toward me through the glass. A hideous face, constructed of many, many hideous pieces.

I stopped moving and shuddered a little bug shudder. What on earth could be so horrifying . . . no, wait, it was just the General. I'd know that mug anywhere. Even bug sight was accurate some of the time.

I ignored him and started to climb once more. This was fun!

I reached the top and stared at the roof of the glass box. Dare I try walking across it?

I stepped out onto it.

I dared.

Huh. This was easy. It was as though gravity had no effect on me. My little, sticky feet carried me across the wide expanse to the far wall, which I then climbed down.

Headfirst. Okay, I admit it. I was a daredevil of a bug.

Something suddenly smacked the glass beside me, knocking me off the wall. Fantastic. But before I could even start to fall, I was suddenly stopped in mid-air. Something on my back had whirred into action and I was floating. I glanced around, trying to focus.

Wings.

Wings? How had I missed those? Oh right. I hadn't been able to make anything out with my hundreds of separate little pieces of vision.

I moved up to the roof and bumped against it a couple of times. Then, as I figured out how my wings worked, I began to control my flight around the inside of my glass prison.

For several minutes, I flew up and down and around. Finally, exhausted, I landed on the wall, high up near the ceiling and rested. I still couldn't make out much in the sight department, but the rest of this tiny body was rapidly becoming mine.

Then I felt the dizziness start to return.

Oh, great. I quickly flung myself into the air and let my tiny wings carry me to the floor. Then I blacked out.

When I came to, I was lying on the little cot, warmly covered by a blanket, with the lieutenant's anxious face over me. I blinked at her and she sighed.

"Oh, good," she said. "You had us worried."

Us? I looked around. She and I were alone in the tiny room.

"The General has gone to get . . ." she swallowed the rest of her words.

"Ummm . . . help?" I hazarded. The idea of the General running for help almost made me laugh. Almost.

She half-smiled.

Footsteps in the hall. Rapid footsteps.

"So what's going on?" My Dad's voice. My Dad was in the hall!

"Dad!" I shouted.

The lieutenant grabbed my shoulders and shoved me back down on the bed. I hadn't realized I had sat up.

"Dad!"

"I'm here, son!" Dad ran into the room. He flung himself down beside me and I wrapped my arms around him. For several minutes, we just hung on. It felt good.

I heard a door close. I looked around. Dad and I were alone in the room. "Well, that was nice of them," I said.

Dad looked up. "What?"

I nodded toward the door. "They've left us alone."

He, too looked around. "Huh. Unexpected." He gave me another squeeze. "It's so good to see you!"

"I've really missed you, Dad."

"And I've missed you, Todd. So much!" Dad let go of me and sat down on the bed. "I just can't believe I'm here with you."

"Me either. How long has it been?"

"64 days."

I felt my eyes widen. "64 days?"

He nodded. "It's inhuman, what they've been doing."

I nodded and reached for his hand. "But we're together now."

He gave my hand a squeeze. "For the moment."

"Yeah."

He rubbed his eyes. "Anyway, I've so much to tell you!"

I sat up.

"Are you okay?" Dad looked at me, concerned.

"I'm fine, Dad."

He sighed. "Good."

"So what's been going on in your life?"

He half-smiled. "You mean apart from being kidnapped and locked into a lab and forced to work on the Essence day and night?"

"Has it been as bad as that?"

Now he did smile. "Not really. They don't overwork me and the food is good."

"Yeah, I can agree with that."

"But I am a prisoner and I was kidnapped." He looked at me. "I suppose you were, too."

"Yeah. They told me that I was brought in for protection and I think they might be right there."

"How so?"

"Well, you remember the experience Orman and I had in the school bus?"

Dad frowned. "I certainly do."

"Well, we think there might have been a second attempt."

"Todd!"

"Yeah. Weird, eh?"

He shook his head. "Go on."

I told him.

"Todd! Are you all right?" Dad reached out and started probing my scalp with gentle fingers.

"Dad, I'm fine! That was 64 days ago!"

He stared at me. "You've been here all this time?"

"I guess so. That afternoon, I was waiting for you at the school and when you didn't show up and I couldn't reach you, I took the bus. We had some sort of mishap with the bus and I . . ." I glanced around, ". . . woke up here."

Dad was silent for a few moments. Finally, "I thought you had just come."

"Nope. Been staying here right along."

He shook his head. "I'm so sorry, son."

"Sorry for what, Dad? Sorry that there are dishonest people in the world who do nasty things to get their way? Sorry that they see the good things you are doing and try to twist them to their own ends?" I shook my head. "Dad, none of this is your fault!"

"My head agrees with you, but . . ."

"I know what you are going to say. And this time, your head is right!"

He smiled faintly.

"So what's your story?" I asked. "How did they drag you down here?"

"Actually, I came on my own two feet." He made a face. "General Doom, I mean Dune, came to talk to me. He said he wanted me to see the lab that his team had assembled and pass judgement on it. I decided, like an idiot, that I could at least do that much for him. I went willingly." His brows gathered into a dark frown.

"And once you got here?"

"Oh, I looked the lab over and made a few suggestions, which they duly noted. Then I told them I needed to leave." He looked at me. "I was worried about being late to pick you up." He sighed. "And that's when the hammer fell. I was 'escorted' by two very large and capable soldiers to my new quarters and locked in."

"Oh, Dad."

"I'll tell you. For the first couple of days, I was so angry at the General that I was incapable of coherent speech. Every time he tried to talk to me, I would end up screaming at him. Many times, I came within a hair's breadth of strangling the man."

I smiled at him. "Well, I'm glad you didn't, Dad."

He snorted.

"Or we would be facing a whole new set of problems."

He laughed. "Too true."

"So you must know where we are."

"That much, I do know," Dad said. "This is a military installation built inside the old mine at Gold Butte."

"In the Sweetgrass Hills?"

"Right."

"Huh. Only a few miles from the ranch."

"Just across the border and east a bit."

"All this time," I said, "we've been almost within spitting distance of home."

Dad nodded.

We were silent for a few moments.

I shrugged. "So, Dad, where's your room?"

"Down here. On the fourth level."

"Really? That's where they've got me!"

He stared at me. "Really?"

"Yeah. I'm in the room directly across from the little monitor station."

"Huh. I'm right at the bottom of the stairs at the end of the hall."

"I can't believe we've been so close." I shook my head. "And all this time . . ." I looked at him. "But they told me that I had to be kept in the 'protected' part of the complex. And that you were in the 'lab' part."

"So?"

"So we are both in the same place. Another lie."

"I think there have been quite a few," Dad said sadly. He summoned up a smile. "At least I know you're all right. I've been so worried . . ."

"Yeah, I'm fine, Dad. I've been spending my days playing Mario or Halo or . . . just loafing."

"Getting your fill of being lazy?"

I grinned at him. "You know I can't believe I'm going to say this, but I miss school."

"And a certain friend at school?"

I felt my face grow hot.

Dad laughed and patted my shoulder. "Don't worry, Son. If it's any comfort, it'll get worse before it gets better . . ."

"Thanks for that."

He laughed again.

"So, Dad, how are we going to get out of here?"

"Well, I've been working on that, son."

"And?"

"I really haven't come up with much. I've been trying to figure a way to use Essence, but they keep every vial locked up tight and very much accounted for."

I grinned at him. "Not like you, Mr. 'I-only-have-one-copy'."

He grinned back. "Definitely not like me." He sobered. "Any escape scenarios I've come up with only included me. Now that I know you are here . . ."

"Yeah. I am a complication."

"Hardly that, son, but I will have to take you into consideration."

"Yeah well, Dad, I'm going to complicate it a bit more."

"What?"

I sighed. "Dad, they've been feeding me the Essence."

Dad stared at me, his face growing red. "Testing it on you."

I nodded. "At almost every meal."

He put his face into his hands. "Oh, Todd, I'm so sorry."

I put a hand on his shoulder. "It's okay, Dad."

He shook his head. "No, son, it's not."

"It really is, Dad."

He looked up at me. "Todd, we really don't know what prolonged exposure will do."

"Well, we're finding out." I leaned back. "Dad, I need to show you something."

"Ummm . . . okay."

I pictured myself as small and furry, with a ringed tail and little, black paws.

Dad scrambled to his feet and stared at me.

"Todd?"

I nodded, then imagined myself. And was once again clutching a blanket to a very human body.

He tottered over to the nearest chair and sank into it. "How . . . how . . ."

"I think it must be a side effect of too much Essence."

"You can change into a racoon whenever you wish?"

"Racoon, tiger, anything I've already been."

"And back again?"

"Instantly."

He blinked. "How . . .?"

"I think that the Essence has done something . . . permanent . . . to me."

"How long have you . . . been able . . .?"

"To change? It's been quite a while now. I've completely lost track of the days."

He scratched his head.

"So . . . days? Weeks?"

I frowned. "Weeks, I think. Certainly more than days."

"Huh."

I grinned. "You're favourite scientific exclamation."

He was silent for several minutes. Finally, "Changing at the molecular level. Could that change one's DNA?" He continued to mumble.

"Dad?"

"Sorry, son. Just trying to get a handle on this."

"Well, let me know when you do."

"You'll be the first . . ." Dad rolled his eyes. "Well, I'd *like* for you to be the first to know." He came back over to the bed and put a hand on my shoulder. "I'll do my best to get us out of this, Todd. My very best."

"Thanks, Dad, I know you will." And I'll be doing a bit of work on it myself.

"Uh, Dr. Iverson?"

Dad didn't move, or even acknowledge that he had heard the lieutenant, who was standing just inside the door.

"Dr. Iverson?"

Dad sighed. "What?"

"I'm afraid it's time for you to go."

Dad looked at her. "Can't stay with my son?"

"It's dangerous for him and for you."

"But, then, why did you . . ."

She came into the room. "We were . . . worried about Todd."

"Why?"

"Well . . . he . . . ingested . . ."

Dad turned his head, fixing an eye on the lieutenant. "You've been feeding him the Essence, haven't you?"

She looked . . . uncomfortable. "Well . . . yes."

"Testing it on him."

She was silent.

Dad turned toward me once more. "There aren't words to describe how despicable I think you are," he said quietly.

The lieutenant's face reddened, but she said nothing.

"To lock up two civilians. Force them to work for you . . ."

"We've done everything for the best of reasons," she said shortly.

"In your eyes."

"So, is Todd all right? He passed out," the lieutenant said.

"What?"

"When he . . . changed back." She looked at me. "You were unconscious."

"Back from what?" Dad was looking at her.

The lieutenant cleared her throat. "You know what he was, Dr. Iverson," she said, quietly.

"You tried the 'fly' Essence on my son?"

"Yes."

Dad closed his eyes. When he opened them, they looked . . . strange. Like . . . cat eyes.

I stared at him.

He blinked and his eyes were normal, once more. I wondered if I had imagined the change.

"Okay," he said, "my impression of you just sank to new levels."

The lieutenant looked down at the floor and shuffled a foot.

"Everything all right?" The General poked his head through the doorway.

The lieutenant looked up. "Umm . . . yes . . . fine," she said.

"Maybe we'd better get them back to their rooms."

Dad stood up. "Yes, by all means, get the prisoners back to their cells."

The General stepped into the room. "You're not prisoners, Dr. Iverson. You're here for your protection."

"Then why can't we be together?"

"Todd is in the protected . . ." the lieutenant started.

"No, don't give us that. We know you have us both here on the fourth floor."

She glanced at the General.

He frowned thoughtfully. "I guess it would be all right for you to spend some time together each day," he said, finally.

My heart gave a leap.

He nodded and put his hands behind his back. "We'll give it a trial period. Every evening for an hour."

"An hour!"

"An hour, Dr. Iverson. That is my only offer."

Dad snorted, then nodded.

The lieutenant cleared her throat. "Umm . . . Dr. Iverson."

Dad sighed. "I know." he said.

Then I realized that Dad's eyes had tears in them. I had never seen my dad cry.

He brushed at his face impatiently.

I slid my legs off the bed and stood up beside him, taking my blanket with me. I glanced at the glass box, still standing in the center of the room. My underwear was sitting in a heap at the bottom. The blanket had been a good idea.

Dad put his arm around my shoulders and gave them a squeeze.

"I'm told this is for the best, son," he said. "But I'm beginning to have my doubts."

"Your son will be well cared for," the lieutenant said, summoning up a smile.

"Yeah, I'm going to trust your word on that," Dad said sarcastically. "You've taken such good care of him so far."

Her face coloured slightly.

Dad looked at me. "I'm so sorry, son," he said softly. "I don't know how to get us out of this, but believe me, I'm working on it."

"Just so long as I know you're all right," I told him, "I'll be just fine."

"That's my boy."

The General, still standing in the doorway, cleared his throat.

Dad squeezed my shoulders again, then dropped his arm. "Fine," he said. "If I must . . ." He winked at me. "See you tonight!" Then he turned to join the General in the hall.

"Dad!" I grabbed his hand.

He turned back. "What is it, son?"

"I love you."

His eyes filled with tears again, but he smiled. "I love you, too, son." Then he pulled his hand away and was gone.

I sat down on the bed, feeling the blackest I had ever felt in my life.

"We'd better get you back to your room, Todd," the lieutenant said.

"Oh, shut up!" I had had enough.

The lieutenant stepped back slightly, surprise on her face. "Now, Todd . . ." She got no further.

"Don't talk to me!" I wrapped my blanket more firmly around my waist and marched out into the hall with her tagging along behind me. I stopped at my door and waited while she unlocked it and swung it open. Then I marched through and shut it in her face.

I leaned back against it until I heard the lock click, then I sank to the floor.

And that's when the tears started.

Chapter Eleven

Sometime later, I scrubbed at my face with the rough blanket and went in search of some clothes. Then I went into the bathroom, my thinking place. I closed the toilet lid and sat down, leaned back against the tank and stared at the blank wall opposite.

I had to get out of here.

And I had to take my dad with me.

Slowly, I began to think. So far, I had been able to change into any animal who's Essence I had ingested.

I focused on what it had been like to become a fly. The smallest of shapes I had been forced into.

Suddenly, I was looking up through a pile of cloth.

I pictured my human self again.

Then sighed and got dressed once more.

Okay. I could manage that easily enough.

Now, what did I know of this place? Its rhythm?

I narrowed my eyes. I was watched in my room, as far as I knew, at every moment of the day or night.

Except Mondays.

Meals were served precisely at the same times each day. 6:00 am, 12:00 noon, and 6:00 pm and, with few exceptions, in the same fashion. The door would open, the tray would be set on the shelf just inside, and the door would close and lock. 15 minutes later, it would be picked up in the same fashion. Depending on where I was in the room, most of the time, I didn't even make eye contact with the bearer.

The other break in my day came at precisely 2:00 pm, when my escort-of-the-moment would shuffle me down the hall to the gymnasium, lock me in, and leave me until 4:00.

And now I would be meeting with my dad for an hour each evening.

Suddenly the isolation that had so chaffed me became a blessing. I realized that I had been left with . . . a lot of time when I could be absent without their knowledge.

I felt the first smile in months on my face.

* * *

"Breakfast!" A voice at my door.

"Wait, I haven't turned the monitors on!" Another voice from out in the hall.

Huh. The monitors weren't on all the time? Another little crumb of information.

"Geeze, I've already got the door open!"

"Well, tell me next time!"

"You can't see me standing here with the tray?"

"Whatever."

I was standing in the doorway of my bathroom, out of direct sight of the main door, which opened away from me.

I glanced over at the bed. I had heaped up the blankets to look as though I was still in there.

"Hey! Sleepyhead! Breakfast!"

I bit my lip. Were they going to actually come in?

"Okay, your funeral." The door smacked shut and the lock clicked.

I let my breath out. So far so good. I could make the breakfast person think I was in my bed. And if the monitors weren't on at night . . .

That gave me the night, after my dad was escorted to his room at 9:00, till breakfast the next day, before my absence would be discovered. Nine hours to explore and come up with possibilities. Tonight would be a good time to start.

I walked over and picked up the tray, setting it on the bed. Mmmm. Scrambled eggs, toast, sausages and a fruit salad.

And the inevitable glass of Essence. Mixed this time with orange juice.

I ate my breakfast, staring all the time at that glass. I had taken to sniffing and tasting the Essence each time, hoping to discover some subtle difference between species. So far, I had detected nothing. Everything tasted and smelled the same.

I tipped up the glass.

* * *

I wasn't sure what I turned into, but it was furry and monkey-like and had little hands that could manage the controllers. It spent the day playing Mario. With the exception of the two hours it was locked into the gym.

Schedules are schedules.

'The Wall' dropped me on the floor of the gym and locked the door. I could hear his footsteps moving away.

This time, I had decided to try an experiment. I pictured . . . Todd. And was instantly sitting, naked, on the cold gym floor. Then I pictured my little, furry self and was just as instantly warmer.

I had made a new and momentous discovery. I could change myself, even if I was still under the influence of Essence.

I tucked this knowledge away with the other bits I was collecting.

I circled the gym, running as hard as this little furry body would allow. Finally, exhausted, I lay down on the floor just inside the door.

'The Wall' opened the door a few minutes later, picked me up, and dumped me on the floor of my room.

I scampered over and switched on the TV. Yep. 4:05. My schedule never varied. I hit the 'hold' button and continued my game where I had left off.

* * *

"Are you sure you want to try this?" Dad was standing beside the door, looking at me.

"Definitely."

He shook his head. "I hope you know what you're doing."

"Dad, I need to know my way around if we expect to be able to get out of here."

"Point taken."

I pulled off my clothes and slid under my blankets. My initial idea of simply arranging my blankets so they appeared inhabited had been scrapped by my father. Instead, we were going to try to show his escort that I was still in my bed, then I would change and make my way out the door when Dad distracted him. Barring complications, it should work like everything always did.

Not.

When the outer door opened a few minutes later, Dad was tucking me in.

"Doc, time to go."

"Yeah, I know." Dad arranged my blanket as I changed. The he straightened and moved toward the door.

"Ouch!" he knocked his shin on the leg of my bed and bent over to rub it.

"Hurry it up, Doc."

"Sorry."

He limped forward.

Meanwhile, a fly zipped, unnoticed, through the opened door and headed up the hall toward the gym.

It worked! I gave a little fly cheer. Okay, it was pathetic, but it was the best I could do.

I was in familiar territory. Even though I still had trouble focusing my eyes in this body, I could manage to

106

navigate. I turned the corner at the gym doors and headed up a hall perpendicular to the one in which I lived. Now the landscape was unfamiliar.

I continued up the hall. More doors. All closed. A sitting room, unoccupied. A library, equally unoccupied.
Wait!
I spun around and headed back to the library. Tall shelves of books divided the otherwise wall-less room. I slid in behind the furthest from the hall and settled onto the floor. For a moment, I caught my little bug breath, then pictured . . . myself.
And was suddenly cold. The coarse, industrial carpet scratched me in places I didn't want to acknowledge. I quickly pictured a dog.
Ahh. Better. I left the library and trotted back up the hall past the gym.
There was a man at the station just outside my room. As I suspected, the monitors were dark. I waited until the soldier had turned away, then crept quietly past toward my dad's room.

* * *

The door was locked.
No surprise.
I sniffed around it, but really had no idea what I was sniffing for. It would take some time spent as a dog for me to get everything figured out. Finally, I scratched at it with my claws.
"Todd, is that you?" Dad's voice came faintly from the inside.
I scratched again.
There was a thump on the door. "Please be careful, son."

I scratched a third time.

"So what are your plans for the evening, Party Man?"

I looked down the hall. A soldier was standing beside the monitor desk.

"Well, I met this new girl . . ."

"Another new girl? Man, Simmons, how do you do it?"

"I'm just a really nice guy."

"Really nice? That does it?"

"Well, really, really nice."

Both men laughed.

I trotted past them and back down the hall.

"Man, Gerrold needs to keep his stupid sniffer dogs with him!" Simmons muttered.

"I'm with you!" the other soldier said.

I spent the rest of the night wandering through the enormous complex.

Most of the doors proved to be locked, but many of the offices had windows facing the hall and I was able to get a good view of their use and whether or not they were occupied. The doors to the stairwells were shut, and though not locked, soon proved to be rather difficult for my doggy paws and awkwardness.

I became a master at running the elevator.

There were four floors in the L-shaped complex. Three of them completely walled off from the outside and very dimly lighted.

And empty of people. Of course I hadn't expected to find more than a skeleton crew because of the time, but I had thought I'd meet . . . someone.

The top floor proved to be above ground. Or at least it had real, outside windows. I put my paws up on the sill and looked out at the night. I hadn't realized until this moment just how much I had missed seeing the sky. I sighed and continued my exploring.

At the end of this hall, light shone out of a set of opened double doors. I trotted toward them and peered inside. Men and a few women, all seated at a large, oval table. I glanced at the intent faces, recognizing only the lieutenant and, at one end, the General.

I moved slowly into the room and curled up under the table.

"So what do you expect me to say?" A man halfway down had risen.

"Well . . ." the General got slowly to his feet. "We've all been working very hard, Major. I just want you to reassure me that you have been working equally hard."

"I haven't even been able to contact my family since I've been here, General," the man said, "because I haven't had time to pick up a phone."

"But what have you accomplished with your time, Major?" the General asked softly.

The Major sighed. "We've been giving the men their Essence," he said finally. "And we've been training each different group in the use of their new skills."

"Good," the General said. "That's all I needed to hear."

Both of them sat down. I stared at the polished shoes so near to me as they shuffled jerkily. The Major wasn't happy.

I glanced around at the various feet. I was getting a distinctly . . . unhappy . . . vibe from the entire group.

"Yes, Lieutenant?"

A woman next to me stood up. "So what are we going to do with them, General?"

I recognized the voice at once. My lieutenant. Or rather the lieutenant who attended me. Or . . . never mind.

There was a general sound of voices agreeing, then silence.

"Do you even know?"

Once more, the General got to his feet. "Well . . ." he began.

Another silence.

"Well?" the lieutenant prompted.

"We . . . haven't decided yet."

"Afraid to push the button?" Another man spoke to my left. I tried to put voice to shoes, then gave up and simply concentrated on what was being said.

"Dr. Sempler, if you were a member of my army, I'd have you court-marshalled for that remark!"

"You haven't answered the question."

"Get out! Get out now!" The voice was a roar. The General's legs were vibrating.

A bit touchy?

"Doesn't change anything," the doctor said as he stood up and moved toward the door. He stopped and turned. "I think you'd better examine your reasons for this operation," he said. "We're trying to save lives. Not take them." He left.

The General sat heavily in his chair.

Another silence fell across those remaining at the table.

"General?" The lieutenant's voice was hesitant. "What do you want to do with them?"

"I'll handle Dr. Iverson and his son," the General said. "It's my responsibility and I knew, going in, that they would become a liability."

Dr. Iverson and his son. A liability. Suddenly, my world didn't look very good.

"So . . .?" the lieutenant prompted.

"I said I'll handle it and I will!" the General's voice rose perceptibly. "Once we've finished with them."

"Very good, Sir." The lieutenant sat down, accidentally kicking me.

I jumped. And yelped. Crap.

110

She peered under the table.

"What is it?" The general asked.

"Just one of Gerrold's dogs."

"What the hell? Someone find Gerrold and tell him to get his dog out of here!"

I got to my feet and stretched. Then sauntered casually out of the room.

Chapter Twelve

From then on, after a much-needed visit with my dad, and with the word 'liability' glowing like a neon sign in my head, I spent my nights frantically exploring.

This building was fairly easy to figure out. Each of the bottom three floors were more or less the same. Long halls with doors at intervals. The occasional alcove with desk or a group of chairs. No windows.

Directly above my gym was another, equally sized room. I had not yet seen inside, but I guessed it probably served the same purpose. I had caught glimpses of soldiers coming and going.

Above that was yet a third large room. The barracks. Row upon row of bunk beds, some occupied during one shift. Some during another. I had spent many hours lying beneath many of those bunks, gleaning information.

"So what are you working next week?"

Two soldiers were sitting on their bunks, talking idly.

"I'm on nights."

"Bummer."

"Jecks, no one says 'bummer' any more."

"Well I do."

"That's because you're ancient." A third voice had joined the other two.

Laughter.

"What have you got, Gerrold?"

"Oh, the usual. Guard duty."

"Pretty choice assignment, I'd say."

"I'm not complaining. 'Course, I don't know what they're going to do about Simmons."

"Still hitting it hard every weekend?"

"Yep."

"I don't know how he gets away with it."

A sigh. "You know Doom never comes in on Mondays."

"Yeah, some sort of meeting."

"Yeah. Sooo . . . that's how Simmons gets away with it. What did you draw, Hatcher?"

"I'm still on the lab."

"That must be sweet."

"It's pretty interesting."

"How did you manage to get that little plum?"

"I've got a degree in microbiology."

"What? No way!"

"Way."

"You never told us that!"

"That's because I didn't think you could even spell 'microbiology', let alone know what it was."

"Well, you've got me there."

Laughter.

Huh. The lab. I still hadn't seen it, though Dad had told me a lot about it. I looked up, trying to peer through the tons of concrete that separated me from the room above this one.

It had to be right up there . . .

* * *

I was exploring the third floor. Somewhere, someone was shouting.

I followed the sound down the hall to the room that corresponded to my gym.

"Come on, men, get your tails in gear!"

The door was slightly ajar. I pushed it with my nose and peered inside.

'Tails' was right. It was a scene straight out of Doctor Doolittle. Or the Ark. Or maybe Dante's Inferno. Animals, groups of them, were working together on different . . . tasks.

A group of bears were trying to construct something out of pieces of wood and fabric. Several large cats, two racoons, and a dozen or so monkeys were climbing about on the huge, wooden frame which filled half the room and reached to the distant ceiling.

I stared at the wooden supports. Something was moving . . . oh . . . snakes, several of them were also making use of the structure.

It was the twisted scene out of a horrid nightmare.

Except that none of the animals were attacking each other. And all seemed to be happily engaged.

I watched two of the cats leap from the climbing frame and chase each other across the hardwood floor.

Yes. Very happily engaged.

"Hey, where's Gerrold?"

A sergeant was walking across the floor toward me.

Oh-oh. I backed up and fled up the hall, scurrying around the corner of a small sitting area just as the door was pushed open.

"Hey, mutt!" There was a pause. "Huh. Can't Gerrold keep his wretched dogs locked up?"

The door closed and I heard the latch click.

I peered around the corner, but the hallway was, once more, deserted. I made my way, unhindered, to the elevator and stabbed the 'up' button with my nose.

The doors slid open silently and I glanced inside.

Empty. I stepped in and was whisked to the top floor.

The doors opened onto an empty hallway. I started down it.

"Hey, hold on a second! It's slipping!" The voice came from just around the corner.

I froze. Then dove behind a small desk sitting against one wall.

114

"Well, get a grip on it! My arms are about to fall off!"

"Okay. Okay, I've got it now."

I peered around the desk.

Two soldiers appeared from the other hallway, carrying a large box. "Okay, just a minute while I get the door."

"Oh, great. You didn't think of opening that before?"

"Keep your shirt on!" The soldier nearest the door shuffled the load to one arm and one knee and fumbled with some keys. Finally, he was able to pull the door open. "There, wimp! That wasn't so bad!"

"For you!"

The two men proceeded through.

I was right behind them.

"Where did the Doc say we were to put this?"

"Just over there, on that table."

My dad's lab. I had finally found it.

Keeping furniture between me and the two soldiers, I made my way over to a bank of windows on one side.

I placed one paw on the sill and stood up on my hind legs, pressing my nose to the thick glass.

Huh. I had expected to look out from a great height, considering I was on the top floor of the complex. But the ground came up right under the window.

Then I realized that this facility had literally been built in the mine. The bottom three floors were deep underground. This, the top floor, was the only portion which stuck out through the top of the hill.

Clever.

I looked through the window. The prairie, lighted by a brilliant three-quarter moon, rolled out away from me, long, dried grasses bending slightly in the breeze. The remaining members of the Sweetgrass Hills stood as dark sentinels around me.

It was a beautiful view. A wonderful place to live . . . unless you are one of those imprisoned in one of the lower floors, I amended to myself.

"Hey, dog!"

I flinched and dropped to the floor, turning my head toward the soldier who had spoken.

"Get out of here!"

I wasted no time.

* * *

During the next few weeks, after I had crept back into my room in the mornings, I caught up on sleep. Then, I played video games and fidgeted until I was escorted to the gym.

Once there, I practiced changing at will. So far, I had been able to change into any animal who's Essence I had ingested.

And, more importantly, change back again.

As the days went past, it got easier and easier. I was able to change back and forth into several animals in the two hours I had.

I was always careful not to change from one directly into another. Visions of a feathered cougar kept me from experimenting very far in that direction.

Just after I reached the gym one afternoon, some sort of alarm began ringing loudly through the entire complex. My escort simply turned me around and trotted me hurriedly back to my room. Just as he opened my door, another soldier appeared and beckoned to us.

"Supposed to take the boy outside," he said.

My escort grunted and continued up the hall. We passed the desk and a couple more doors. The other soldier had paused beside Dad's door and was unlocking it.

My escort paused.

116

"Keep moving!" the other soldier barked.

My escort gave me a shove and we continued up the hall.

I glanced back just as my dad emerged.

"Dad!" I shouted.

He looked up. "Todd!"

My escort shoved me hard and I fell to my knees. When I regained my feet, my father and his escort were nowhere to be seen. I kept glancing behind me as I was pushed forward, but I didn't see him again. We reached the end of the hall and a set of heavy, metal doors I had always found to be locked.

My escort pulled out his keys and inserted one into the lock.

It was then that I realized something. Though there were several keys on his ring, only one was black. I had seen it used multiple times to open both my room door and the door to the gym.

I had thought nothing of it.

Now that same black key was being used to open this door. Huh. All the doors opened with the same key.

Security here stank.

The door swung open to reveal a staircase and a small elevator. My escort chose the elevator. I glanced at his broad girth. Why was I not surprised?

It opened. We got in and he punched 'G'. The elevator shot upwards, stopping with a jerk. The door slid open and we stepped outside into warm sunshine. And a large group of . . . soldiers.

At least, I tried to imagine they were soldiers.

Four huge bears were sitting together, sunning themselves just outside the doors. Beside them, also enjoying the early afternoon sun, were a dozen or so large, black cats and four racoons. All of them turned to look at me.

117

Surreal.

The elevator slid open behind me and I turned to see a soldier, real, this time, carrying a large box and being followed by several monkeys. He set his box on the ground and I saw a snake raise its head and make its way over the side. Another followed.

Okay. Beyond surreal. Now it was just weird.

"Now don't try anything," 'The Wall said.

I looked at the animals watching me and shook my head. 'Trying something' was definitely not on the agenda at the moment.

"Follow me."

I obeyed immediately.

He led me along a path worn in natural grassland to a small, stone structure, then stepped back. "Inside, please."

I paused in the doorway and peered into the darkness.

He snorted audibly and gave me a rough shove. I stumbled across a stone threshold and into the cool, dark room, banging my shin painfully against something. The door swung shut behind me and I heard a lock snap.

Sigh.

I stood there and waited for my eyes to accustom themselves to the gloom. Finally, I was able to make out my surroundings. This must be their storage shed. The space was taken up by various gardening implements and machines. I stared at a riding lawnmower. Why on earth was that here? Where would they use it? I smiled as I pictured it as a getaway vehicle.

Yeah. No.

Light was filtering into the room from the far wall. I carefully edged closer. A window was almost completely covered by a heavy, wooden shutter. I pushed on it. It was bolted shut from the outside.

I leaned closer, trying to see through the cracks. Something moved across the window outside and I jumped back, startled. Then I shook my head. Get a grip, Todd!

I approached the window once more and peered through the widest crack. A face was staring back at me. A large, tawny cat face. It winked. I handled the shock in my usual cool, manly fashion.

I screamed.

Chapter Thirteen

The face disappeared.

I pressed my eye to the crack. Nothing. The empty, silent landscape stretched away from me to the purple hills in the distance.

What on earth? I sat down on the mower and put my chin in my hands. Had that really been Rich? But how could he know where I was? And more importantly, how had he avoided detection?

Suddenly, a twist of paper appeared through the crack in the window. I stared at it. Then jumped to my feet and fell over a rake. Todd, the clod, in action once more.

Finally, reaching the window, I grabbed the paper and once more pressed my eye to the crack. A long, tawny form dropped to the ground a short distance away. It blended almost perfectly with the dried, yellow grasses. Huh. So that's where he had gone.

I opened the note.

JoJo's hurried scrawl. "We weren't sure if this would work. We've managed to stop up the exhaust system temporarily. That is what set off the alarm. We're working on a plan. Ideas?"

Dad and I had help. My mind began to work frantically. How could we use them? We'd have to get to a spot in the building where they could help us get out . . .

The lab! It had windows. Now if I could just get there when my dad was there.

The answer was suddenly clear. Mondays. When the monitors were shut off. I would have all morning to get to the lab before I was discovered. Hopefully by then, Dad and I would be specks in the distance.

There were definitely a lot of things that could go wrong. I knew that he had other people working with him.

Well, we'd just have to see what we could work out.

I searched frantically through the gloom for something to write with. Nothing. Wait. There was a small iron stove in the corner, a rusted stovepipe poking crookedly through the roof.

I swung the door back. Old ashes. I scrambled through them, finally picking up a small, partially-burned piece of wood.

I spread out the paper and wrote, "Lab. Monday A.M. Bring coyote Essence." Then carefully rolled the paper, poked it back through the crack and wiggled it. Then I pulled it back and took a look.

The tawny shape rose up out of the grass and looked around. Then it moved quickly toward me.

I poked the paper through again. Further this time. It disappeared.

Our escape plan was underway.

* * *

"So what do you think?"

Dad frowned thoughtfully. "It just might work, son."

I smiled. "Finally, some good news."

Dad walked over to my entertainment unit and leaned an elbow on it. Then he turned to look at me and nodded. "Yes. It just might work."

"So I'll get out of my room when they come to pick up the tray and wait outside the door of your lab until you get there."

"Sounds good. Then the two of us can break a window, Rich and JoJo can pass us the Essence. We change and we leave." Dad smiled at me. "Well, at least I take the Essence and change. You're on your own."

I smiled back. "Simple and perfect."

"Yes. Except for Hatcher."

"Hatcher?"

"My assistant."

"Oh."

Dad shook his head. "Well, we'll just have to play the hand as it comes."

I nodded. "I don't know what else we can do."

"Hatcher will have to be immobilized . . . somehow."

"Immobilized."

We stared at each other.

Finally, Dad shrugged. "Well, let's just hope that we don't have to hurt him."

I raised my eyebrows and nodded. "Oh, Dad, one last thing."

"What's that?"

"What day is it?"

He grinned. "Saturday, Todd. We have one day to prepare."

* * *

I spent most of Sunday going over and over our little plan. One minute it seemed foolproof. The next, stupid. By the time Dad was ushered in, I had almost given up on it.

"It'll work, Son," he said, patting my shoulder. "Now, you know what you're going to do?"

"Pretty much."

"Good. Now stop thinking about it!"

I snorted. "I'll try." I make no promises.

* * *

That night, I stayed in my room. I told myself that exploring was a waste of time when we'd be leaving the next day.

But I didn't sleep. I spent the time changing back and forth into different animals.

122

It kept me entertained and at least stopped my thinking.

* * *

"Breakfast!"

I turned over and looked at the door, just catching the soldier's eyes.

"Breakfast," he repeated.

I nodded. "Thanks."

He set my food down on the floor and closed the door.

I stared at the tray. My stomach was tied in such knots that I doubted I would be able to swallow anything. But I probably needed to eat.

I managed to get most of the eggs and bacon down, but the toast merely stuck in my throat.

I gulped down the Essence and hardly noticed when I became small and feathered. I opened my mouth and let out a trill of notes. Huh. For the first time in my life, I could sing. I flew into the bathroom and tried my best to hover beside the mirror. A canary. Cute.

I heard the door to my room open. Here for the tray already?

"Todd?" The General's voice.

My heart stopped. Okay, the plan was getting off to a rocky start.

Chapter Fourteen

I flew out of the bathroom and landed on the top of my entertainment unit.

"Oh, there you are." The General was standing just inside my door. He smiled. "Just wanted to check up on you."

Well, I'm doing just fine, thank you. And what are you doing here? You're supposed to be in meetings with other military types. I glanced past him into the hall.

The desk was manned and all the monitors were on. Crap. Okay, okay, don't panic, Todd. We can still make this work.

My little birdie brain was thinking frantically.

The bathroom. There were no monitors in the bathroom. If I could make them think I was in there . . . It wouldn't give me a lot of time, but it might still work.

I looked one last time at the general, then headed deliberately back into the bathroom.

"Well, I won't keep you, son. Just wanted to check up."

Yeah, yeah. I perched on the toilet and glanced behind me. The bathroom doorway remained empty. I changed for an instant into myself, then into a fly.

And just managed to slip through the closing door behind the general.

Okay, that was a little too close. If I'd had a tail . . .

"How's he been doing?" The general paused beside the desk.

The guard leaped to his feet and saluted. "Fine, sir."

"Any changes?"

"Well, he does seem to be in a bit better spirits since he has been seeing his father."

"Good. Good. Carry on."

"Yes, sir."

I followed the general up the hall at a discrete distance. No sense getting myself swatted. That would end things very quickly.

And permanently.

He unlocked the doors leading to the outside elevator and closed them behind him. Good. That was one complication out of the way.

But I still needed to hurry. I glanced down the hall. Deserted. I settled on the floor and changed briefly into myself, then back into my dog. I pushed the button to call the elevator.

A short time later, I was sitting outside the door of Dad's lab.

"So, when is she due?"

"Oh, she still has a couple of months."

Three soldiers left the elevator and came toward me down the hall.

I stayed where I was.

At any other time, the soldiers stationed here ignored 'Gerrold's dogs'.

"Hey. There's another of your stupid dogs!"

"Get him!"

Things were definitely not going according to plan. I turned and dashed up the hall away from them.

"Come here, you stupid mutt! I'm going to beat you senseless!"

Yeah, that makes me want to run to your arms.

Not.

I dashed into a small alcove. I had only seconds.

A hand grabbed me by the skin of my neck.

Okay, less than seconds.

I sighed. What else could go wrong?

"What should we do with him, Gerrold?"

"I'll just lock him in the kennel with the others."

"How on earth did he get out?"

125

"I have no idea," Gerrold said. "Unless he got past the boy when he was feeding this morning."

"You know, I think this is the same dog I've seen wandering around before."

"Well, obviously, he's smarter than the others."

Smarter? Huh. That's not a term I've had applied to me before. For a moment, I felt the stirrings of pride. No, wait. I'm a dog. I'm being compared to other dogs. Okay. Pride gone.

Gerrold dragged me down the hall and paused before a locked door. He reached into his pocket and produced a key. "Here. Could you open up?"

"Sure." The soldier unlocked the door and swung it wide. Instantly, we could hear the yapping and barking of several dogs.

"Good thing that room's sound proof," the soldier with the key said.

"Yeah. Otherwise they'd drive us all nuts!"

I was pulled inside.

"Ralf, grab me one of those collars."

The third soldier reached into a bundle of leather straps hanging from a hook and tightened one around my throat.

Okay. Okay. That's tight enough . . .

"Loosen it a bit, would you, Ralf?" Gerrold laughed. "He's starting to look a bit bug-eyed."

The pressure was slackened. I took a deep, appreciative breath.

"Good."

"So what do you want to do with him?"

"We'll just put him back into his . . . huh."

"What is it?"

"Well, all of the kennels are full."

"So?"

"Well, each of my dogs is kennelled separately. It saves on a lot of hassle."

"Yeah?"

"So this can't be one of my dogs."

There was silence for a moment. "So where did it come from?"

"I don't know. But I'm going to find out." Still keeping a tight hold on my collar, Gerrold grabbed a leash and snapped it on. "I'll just tie him here and we'll go and find out who he belongs to."

"And just what he's doing in a military instillation in the middle of nowhere."

Gerrold tied the leash to the corner of the nearest kennel and turned toward the door.

"You know all of this is using up valuable drinking time," Ralf said. "I've just come off a really boring night shift and I want my after-work breakfast beverage."

"Well, it shouldn't take too long." Gerrold smacked Ralf on the back. "Let's go."

All of my days of practice were suddenly put to use. In a flash, I had changed into a fly. I buzzed frantically toward the door.

It shut in front of me.

Crap.

For several minutes, and ignoring the din of barking, howling animals, I crept around the outer edges of the door, looking for an opening. Finally, I settled onto the wall just over the door and sighed. Obviously, soundproof also meant air tight.

I glanced around. But it couldn't be airtight with all of these dogs in here. I took off again, keeping close to the ceiling and looking for any possible openings.

There. A vent. I buzzed over to it. Cool air was blowing through a fitted cover. Battling the light breeze, I climbed inside.

I found a heavy screen, just big enough to admit my little buggy body. I took a deep breath and shoved my way through.

Ouch.

Once inside, the breeze was considerably stronger, at least for my tiny fly muscles. I clung to the slippery galvanized steel and tried to inch my way along.

I had made some progress, a mile or so in fly feet, but probably about six inches in reality, when the breeze suddenly . . . picked up.

And took me with it. I hit the wall on the other side of my vent.

Sigh. This wasn't working very well. If only I were larger. Even slightly.

I glanced around. There was no way this small area would be big enough for my human self.

I started to crawl back down toward the 'floor' of the shaft.

Then a thought struck me. When Gerrold and his cronies had been leaving the kennel, I had frantically changed into a fly. Had I taken the time to change into myself first? I stopped where I was and tried to think.

Had I?

I didn't think so.

Maybe I could change from one animal to another. Maybe.

I licked my foot and rubbed it over my head.

Ewww! What was I doing?

I had obviously been in this body long enough.

My decision was made. I pictured a racoon.

* * *

I opened my eyes.

Okay, eye opening was a good sign.

128

I looked down. Furry little hands. Furry little feet. A ringed tail.

It had worked!

I didn't need to change into myself before changing into something else. Another little tidbit of discovery!

I wasted no more time, but started down the shaft, making considerably more progress than my fly self had made.

The large shaft I was following branched ahead of me. I paused in the opening. Which way to go?

I decided that my best solution would be to follow the line that seemed to head toward the lab. Maybe I would get lucky. Like I had been so far.

Right.

The shaft branched again. I paused and looked right and left. Then I shook my head and turned into the left line.

Maybe it would at least take me back to the hallway .
. .

Another vent! I paused over it and looked through. Just as two soldiers walked beneath it.

I drew back, then, realizing that they really weren't looking in my direction, and probably couldn't see me if they were, leaned forward once more.

Definitely the hallway. I had made a 'U' circuit almost back to where I had started. I imagined a fly and slipped between the screen over the vent.

Just as a loud siren began to blare.

Chapter Fifteen

I raced up the hall, finally coming to rest on the
ceiling just over the lab door.

"Well, I can't figure it out!" Gerrold was shaking his
head as the three soldiers came out of the kennel. He turned
to Ralf. "Are you sure . . ."

"You saw me!" Ralf said indignantly. "I put the collar
on!"

"And I tied the thing!" Gerrold said.

"There's something really strange going on around
here," Ralf said

"Look around, guys!" the third soldier said.
"Everything around here is really strange!"

There was a pause. "Do you suppose that we tied up
one of our buddies?" The other two stared at Gerrold.

"I never even though of it," Ralf said. "But that still
doesn't explain what he was doing here. Or where he went."

"You're right." Gerrold sighed. "Well, we might as
well start looking."

Rolf moaned.

"Oh, come on. We can drink later!"

The three of them hurried up the hall.

I dropped to the floor and changed into human shape.
Then I pushed open the door.

"Todd! Thank heaven! I was really starting to get
worried!"

"Hi, Dad." I looked down. A soldier lay sprawled on
the floor, unconscious. His arms had been secured with
duct tape. His legs as well.

"Wow! Dad!"

He shook his head. "Hurry, there's no time to lose!"
he said, pushing the door shut behind me and twisting the
heavy lock.

"Here, help me."

The two of us pushed a metal table over against the door and wedged it as tightly as we could against several other pieces of furniture.

"Someone's set off the alarm," Dad grunted as he worked, "I think they've discovered something."

"Yeah. My absence." I smiled at him and pictured a coyote.

Dad hurried to the window and picked up a heavy piece of metal lying on the counter. Swinging his improvised club with both hands, he hit the heavy glass. It cracked.

Just then, I saw a figure standing on the grass outside. A cougar. I moved to stand beside my father.

He swung the bar again. This time, the thick glass shattered, spraying tiny bits everywhere.

The cougar ducked to one side, then immediately moved toward us and dropped a small, cloth bag on the windowsill.

Dad grabbed it and reached inside and pulled out two vials of coyote Essence. He dropped one vial back inside, then stuffed the bag into a backpack. Then he stripped off his pants and shirt and stuffed them into the backpack as well. Finally, he put on the backpack, snapped the end off one vial and tipped up the contents.

I watched as he changed.

Suddenly, something heavy hit the door of the lab. Startled, the two of us turned. The door shivered under the impact of another blow.

Dad looked at me and jerked his head toward the window. I nodded and leaped through the opening.

The cougar batted at me with a soft paw. The two of us turned to see Dad clear the window, then we all started off down the hill.

The cougar moved out in front and led us at a fast pace.

131

I heard a yelp behind me and skidded to a stop, turning just as Dad completed a somersault, landing on his belly with all four legs splayed. Another yelp.

I hurried toward him but two panthers got there first. The four of us looked at each other. I could see the muscles twitch under smooth, black skin.

Oh, man.

I didn't stop to think it through. If I had, I probably wouldn't have done it. I leaped forward.

Now, I'm not really sure if ever, in the history of the world, a coyote has attacked a panther. Or panthers. But it did now.

And I'm pretty sure it wasn't what the two big cats expected. They leapt apart and I came down in the middle, almost on top of Dad.

By this time, he had managed to scramble to his feet. Then the cougar joined us.

The three of us charged forward, two coyotes taking one panther. The cougar taking the other. This time, though, the panthers were ready and they stood their ground.

I should explain, here that panthers outweigh coyotes by . . . a fair amount. We two coyotes merely . . . bounced off. Rather humiliating to admit, but, there you are.

Fortunately for our side, the cougar was a bit more intimidating. It brought claws into play, slashing down the ribs of the other panther as it landed.

The stricken animal screamed and leaped back, obviously wanting no more of the fight.

Its companion glanced over, then grabbed Dad by his back pack and gave him a toss, swatted me away like a pest and charged the cougar.

Dad went down hard. I heard the air 'whoosh' as it left him. I was torn between helping the cougar and defending Dad. For just a second, I looked from one to the other.

Either way, I needed to be . . . bigger. Bear, I thought. Instantly, I felt my body swell in size and mass.

Just then, the panther raked razor claws through the air, and slashed the cougar across one thigh. My decision was made. I charged the panther.

I never reached it.

The cougar had made no sound, but spun around gracefully; claws extended, and went for the other animal's eyes.

The panther ducked and the swing went wide, but the intent was perfectly clear. This fight was deadly serious. The second panther backed away toward its companion and the two of them retreated up the hill.

I changed into a coyote and ran toward my dad, but the cougar was there first, nosing at him. Dad slowly got to his feet. Then he shook himself and started running once more.

I breathed a sigh of relief and quickly fell into step behind him. The cougar moved once more into the lead.

Then I heard the scream of an eagle.

I glanced up, just as a beautiful bird sailed past me, heading back toward the complex. I looked behind.

The panthers had been joined by another large, striped cat and were once more heading down the hill toward us.

The eagle dove at the striped one, raking at it eyes with deadly claws. The cat swerved, changing course dramatically.

'Way to go!' I said to myself. Then turning back, I redoubled my efforts and was soon running alongside my father. He, too had seen the eagle and he looked at me and raised his . . . eyebrows.

I nodded.

A feline scream behind us let us know that our friend, the eagle, was still making itself very much known.

We reached the bottom of the hill and the cougar started out across the prairie. It seemed to be leading us toward the next hill a couple of miles away.

We had managed maybe half of the distance, when I noticed that Dad was panting and showing signs of slowing.

Oh, great.

I was seriously beginning to worry that he wouldn't be able to keep up when the cougar disappeared into a fold in the prairie.

Dad and I put on a burst of speed and followed. Just over the rise, we saw a tiny opening in the side of a small hummock of ground. At first glance, it appeared too small to admit either Dad or I, and certainly not big enough for all three of us. But as the cougar disappeared inside, I realized that it was much, much roomier than it appeared.

Dad and I both charged inside, sliding to a halt a short distance from the entrance. I looked around. We were obviously inside another entrance to the mine. Old timbers stood solidly about us and the ground sloped radically and almost immediately into inky blackness.

The cougar was standing just at the edge of the drop-off. I moved closer and bumped it with my nose. It swatted me with a paw.

And then Rich was sitting there, blinking at us.

A naked, shivering Rich.

I blinked. Rich? Then the eagle was . . .?

"Man, I was getting a bit worried," he said. He moved closer to the wall and pulled a backpack out of the shadows. "I didn't have much time left and I was starting to think I'd have to come back here and take another dose." He upended the pack, spilling out folded clothes and some packets of food and bottled water.

"These are for you, when you are yourselves again," he said. He pulled on a pair of fleece pants and a hoodie.

I pictured myself. "So JoJo's the eagle?"

Rich's head popped out of the hoodie and he stared at me. "Wow. That was fast! I didn't expect to be able to talk to you for some time yet."

I smiled and reached for some clothes. "I'm a quick healer."

He nodded. "I would say so." He looked at Dad, but Dad only shook his head and sat down and sighed. He would have to wait.

"So . . . Hi!" Rich said. "And yeah. To answer your question, JoJo's the eagle. Wasn't that exciting?!"

"Well, I don't know if 'exciting' is the word I'd use, but I've never been so glad to see anyone in my whole life, Rich. And good work out there, by the way."

He grinned. "Well, I have to say that was a bit more of an adventure than JoJo and I were counting on, but I'm glad I could be of help."

"How's your leg?"

He looked down, surprised. "Geeze, I forgot all about it."

"Doesn't it hurt?"

He shrugged. "Not a bit."

"Weird."

"Totally." He looked toward the entrance. "So, who were those guys?"

"The ones in the black pajamas?"

"Yeah."

I shrugged. "I figure they must be soldiers."

"Not really ready for a fight, were they?"

"Yeah, I was glad that they seemed to poop out so quickly." I grinned at him. "Between you and me, I really wasn't ready for a fight, either."

He looked at me for a moment. "There was a bear," he said.

"What?"

135

"There was a bear."

I felt my face redden. "You're imagining things."

He shook his head, but didn't say anything more.

"Sooo . . . how did you find us?"

"Well, actually, I can't claim much of the glory for that," he said. "Mostly, it was JoJo. She just wouldn't give up."

"Jo?"

"Yeah. She was pretty worried about you. She figured that you had been kidnapped."

"Makes sense," I said. "With Dad and I both disappearing, it is a logical conclusion."

"Exactly." Rich looked at me. "Anyway, it turns out that Jami's dad is ex-military. A major or something like that."

"Really? How come we didn't know that?"

"I asked Jami the same thing. She says they don't talk about it much. She said something about 'JTF', whatever that means."

"Joint Task Force," I said.

"Oh, you know?"

"Yeah. One of the few things I do know." I grinned at him. "They're Canada's answer to the CIA or special forces or something like that."

"Huh. Well, anyway, I guess he still has some contacts somewhere. Jami was talking to her parents about you and your dad, and how worried we all were. Then, afterwards, she overheard her dad telling her mom that the military installation in the Sweetgrass Hills had become active. He was wondering if it had anything to do with your disappearance. Apparently, this place had been sitting here practically empty for years."

He shrugged. "Anyway, Jami obviously couldn't ask her father for more information, so JoJo started taking flights over the hills to see if she could spot anything. It

136

didn't take her long to see that one of the back roads was being used regularly. After that, all she had to do was follow the tire tracks. They led her right here."

"Sounds pretty simple when you lay it all out from start to finish."

"Yeah. Like Sherlock Holmes."

"Right, Rich. Whenever I think of you, I think of Sherlock Holmes!"

Rich laughed. "So, as it turns out, Jami's dad was right."

"About . . .?" I had lost the thread of the conversation.

"About who kidnapped you. It was the military."

"Yeah, General Dune, or Doom as Dad calls him. To hear him tell it, we were taken for our own protection. And, you know, thinking about the bus and the change room incidents, I think he was right."

"Well, JoJo and I think it was him or his cronies who were behind those as well. So that you'd think you needed protection."

"Really?"

"Yeah."

"Huh." I raised my eyebrows and looked at Dad.

He was staring at Rich. Then he turned and looked at me. Slowly, he nodded.

My heart stopped.

"You think Doom was scaring us so we'd come to him?"

He nodded again.

"What a jerk!"

Dad's coyote mouth stretched wider, almost a grin.

"So what do we do now?"

"We wait till your Dad changes," Rich said. He held out his hand and opened it. Four vials clicked together softly. "Your Uncle Peter has been keeping us supplied."

I leaned forward.

Eagle. My favourite.

"You want us to escape as eagles?"

He grinned. "There's no way they can track us as eagles."

I nodded. "You have a point."

"Can't they track us here, Rich?"

Dad's voice. Rich and I turned.

"Oh, Dr. Iverson. You're back!"

"I am. So can't they? Track us, I mean."

"Well, there are animal tracks all over here, some from wild animals, but most of them from soldiers learning how to use their animal bodies. There are tracks from big cats, dogs, coyotes, wolves. Any of which would confuse them and make them lose our trail. And as far as we've been able to discover, no one has quite figured out how to use their animal noses yet, so I think we're okay."

Dad nodded. "Even so, we should probably get started immediately." He reached for one of the vials that Rich was still holding out.

"We have to wait for JoJo," Rich said, closing his hand.

"Oh," Dad shook his head. "Right. I wasn't thinking."

He slipped out of his backpack. Then he grabbed his clothes and pulled them on as he walked toward the opening. He leaned forward and peered out. "Any idea when she'll get here?"

"Well, it had better be soon, or she'll be out of time," Rich said. "I'm sure her hour is almost up."

Dad turned. "What's your contingency plan?"

"Well, we didn't have one," Rich looked uncomfortable. "The plan was for her to watch from the top of the hill until I got the two of you away, then change into an eagle and guard our back trail."

Dad pursed his lips. "Sounds reasonable."

"We figured, as an eagle, she would be able to stay up, out of danger."

I joined Dad at the opening. "Any sign of her?"

He scanned the sky between us and Gold Butte. "No."

My heart suddenly felt like lead. "Something's wrong."

Chapter Sixteen

Half an hour later, JoJo still hadn't returned.
I stripped off my clothes.
Dad threw out his hand. "Wait, Todd!" he said. "We need a plan."
"I'm just going to have a look around." I closed my eyes and pictured an antelope.
When I opened them again, Rich was staring at me, wide-eyed.
"T, how did you . . .?"
I didn't wait for him to finish. I was through the mine entrance in one leap.

* * *

There was a lot of activity around the entrance to the complex.
Soldiers, human this time, were milling about just outside the doors. Several of them had binoculars and were scanning the countryside. For several minutes, I watched them from behind a convenient, and very lonely, bush.
Then I slowly wandered forward.
They spotted me almost immediately. I saw several pairs of binoculars lowered and pointing fingers.
I kept my nose close to the ground as though I was grazing.
They studied me for a few minutes. Then they must have decided that I was the real thing, because they seemed to lose interest.
I moved as close as I dared. There was no sign of an eagle. Or of a girl with long, dark hair.
Sigh.

Suddenly, I spotted movement at the very top of the hill. Where the windows protruded. A man slowly stood up. Then he lifted something.

A bow!

My heart stopped. Was this the reason JoJo hadn't returned? Had she been wounded?

Killed?

Suddenly the hottest anger I had ever known shot through me. A red haze seemed to cloud my sight. I wanted to smash something! Kill something! For several seconds, I stood stock still. Trembling.

I took a deep breath. Another. Finally, my vision cleared and my thought processes slowed down to a manageable pace. Okay. So JoJo wasn't in sight, either as an eagle or a girl. Okay. That didn't necessarily mean that she had been killed. Or even captured. There were many, many possible reasons why she hadn't returned.

I moved back behind my bush and thought for a minute. Probably the best way for me to get information would be to get closer. Good thinking, Todd. Closer. That would mean something . . . smaller.

A few seconds later, a gopher was nosing its way toward the complex entrance.

* * *

The sun was getting hot. I glanced up at it through the screen of dried grass. Must be nearly noon.

Most of the soldiers had gone inside. Only a couple, armed with binoculars, were still sitting outside the entrance.

"How did we manage to draw this detail?" one of them asked.

"Luck, I guess."

141

"I don't know why they want us to keep watching. Dr. Iverson and his son are long gone."

The second soldier snorted. "Now I know why you were chosen for this detail."

"What?"

"Lutz, you're an idiot!"

"How so?"

The second soldier sighed. "They want us to keep watching because we have the girl."

"Yeah, but she's inside."

He sighed again. "Right, but they think that Iverson and son will try to get her out."

"Oh. Right. Never thought of that."

"Obviously."

"So how long do we have to stay here?"

"Till the end of our shift."

"Well I'm hot." Lutz stood up. "Want a drink? I'm buying."

"Are you nuts?"

"Water, Jacobs, water. I'll get you a bottle, too."

"Oh. Okay. Thanks."

Lutz disappeared inside the building.

I had learned two things. One, that JoJo was alive. And two, that she was a prisoner.

We needed to make some plans. I hurried back to our hideout as fast as my little gopher legs would take me.

* * *

"I'm afraid it will all be up to you, son," Dad said.

"I agree. I'm the only one who can change on the fly. Ummm . . . no pun intended."

"Getting in will be no problem," Dad went on. "You will only have yourself to worry about. But getting out . . ." he didn't finish.

142

He didn't have to.

For the past hour, the three of us had been conceiving and discarding plans. Now we were back to zero. And still not knowing what we could do to get JoJo out.

"So, getting in and out poses . . . problems. What about doing the opposite?" I said.

Dad and Rich turned to look at me. "Go on, son," Dad said.

"Well, what can we do that will bring them . . . out?" I asked.

"Could we set off the alarm again?" Rich asked.

"What did you do the last time?"

"JoJo discovered the exhaust for the heating/cooling system and built a nest in it."

Dad nodded and smiled. "Clever girl."

"It took them a while to find it, but once they did, they dismantled it pretty fast." He suddenly paused. "Huh."

"What is it?" Dad asked.

"Well, I wonder now if her little scheme didn't backfire. I wonder if that was why there was a man prowling around with a bow and arrow. To keep any wandering birds from building another nest."

Dad shrugged. "Could be."

"Well, it really doesn't matter now, anyway," Rich said. "Except that I don't think we can try that again."

"So what will work?" I asked.

"Now? Probably only a natural disaster," Rich said.

Dad suddenly looked thoughtful. "Well, that's an idea," he said.

"You can call up a natural disaster?" I asked him.

Dad smiled. "Well, think about it, boys. Name some natural disasters."

"Okay. Umm . . . floods. Tornados. Earthquakes. Cyclones. Hurricanes." Disasters were something I knew a lot about.

"Volcanoes. Fires. Droughts. Plagues. Infestations. "
Rich had obviously been reading the same books I had.

"Wait!" Dad said. "That's it!"

We both stared at him.

"You want us to come up with an infestation?" I
could probably do one bug. But millions . . .?

"No. Fire! That we can do!"

"Dad. We can't start a fire."

"Why not?"

"Well, for one thing, once you start it, there's no way
you'll ever control it."

"We'll start a little one."

"Dr. Iverson, that sounds good, except how do you
keep it a little one?" Rich was talking to empty space
because Dad had stepped outside.

Rich and I moved to the doorway and stood,
watching him.

He stuck a finger in his mouth and then held it up.
"Hmmm . . . wind's from the west, as usual. Not very high,
for a change. Dried grass." He looked around. "No
development directly east." He nodded. "Yes. This just
might work."

He ducked back into our cave and grabbed his
backpack. "Matches," he mumbled, "grass will probably
do."

"Dad?"

He ignored me. Just kept talking to himself and
pulling stuff out of his backpack.

"Dad, think about it."

He sifted through a sheaf of papers and finally
pounced on a book of matches. "Ha! I knew I had put them
in there!"

He turned to Rich and I. "Okay. Here's what we'll do.
Todd, you change into a gopher and move to the other side
of the compound. Then you change into whatever animal

144

can actually light the matches and set a fire along the road coming in, as close as possible to the compound." He took a deep breath. "Hopefully, they will think that it was caused by a carelessly thrown cigarette."

He rubbed his forehead. "The alarm will go out quite quickly. We have to be prepared for anything."

"But how do we get to JoJo?" Okay, I was fairly single-minded at the moment.

"They will bring her out and either lock her into the shed or put her right into a vehicle. One of us will have to get a vial of eagle Essence to her somehow."

"It sounds like a lot will depend on 'somehow', Dad."

"I know, son, but we need to get JoJo out and this is the best we can do at the moment."

I thought about all of the possible scenarios we had discussed over the past hour, then nodded. He was right.

"So what do we have for supplies?"

"Well, we have one vial of unused coyote Essence because Todd thinks he's now 'super-change guy' or something."

I grinned at him. "Just 'super guy', Rich."

Rich rolled his eyes and grinned back. "And we have the four vials of eagle."

"Okay. Todd won't need any of that, so he can carry one eagle vial and Rich and I can carry the other. Then whichever group can, will get it to her."

"I'll make sure the fire is going well, then I'll make my way back to the entrance and wait there," I said. Oh please let it be me who saves her, I thought. Please. Please. Please.

"Lucky for us there is only one entrance," Dad said.

"At least as far as JoJo and I were able to discover," Rick said. "You have to keep in mind that this is a mine and that there may be other entrances just as hidden as this one we're standing in."

145

Dad nodded. "Point taken. Well. Are we ready?"

"As much as we ever will be," I said. Super-change guy . . . ready to . . . super-change.

"Let's get started."

* * *

I untangled myself from Rich's small, cloth bag that Dad had tied around me and pulled out the matches, quickly discovering that gophers, even if they have cute little 'hands', lack the necessary skills to actually strike a match.

Racoons, however, suffer no such difficulties.

I soon had a small fire going.

Which quickly caught in the tall, dry grass and became a big fire.

Great.

I raced along ahead of it, but was only half-way up the hill when I heard the blare of the alarm. And something else I hadn't counted on; the thump of heavy army boots as soldiers boiled out of the entrance, paused a moment to glance around, then charged down the hill.

Towards me.

Double great.

Frantically, I searched for a place to hide. There! A real gopher's hole. I didn't pause, just changed into a gopher and made a leap into it. Darkness closed around me. The smell was, at once, earthy and musky.

And dusty.

I held my breath as many sets of footsteps pounded past me and on down the hill. Then, something in front of me . . . squeaked.

Do gophers get angry? Because it sounded, distinctly, like an angry squeak.

146

More squeaks. I could now make out a couple of pairs of eyes ahead of me in the tiny gopher throughway. Eyes that didn't blink. And didn't look very happy, either.

Reverse gear was needed. Quickly.

I backed out of the tunnel and into the light. Better the evil you know, right? But no footsteps pounded past me. I glanced down.

Everyone was at the bottom of the hill, shovelling and throwing dirt and beating at the flames with gunny sacks.

I scurried the rest of the way up the hill, and hunted for the little vial I had hidden beside the building's entrance on my way to start my little fire. Then I peered cautiously around the corner of the building toward the entrance to see what was happening.

There was only one soldier visible. Standing directly outside the little storage hut that had been my home such a short time ago. Good. They must have put JoJo in there. That made things easy.

For once.

I could see a couple of shadows moving around on the far side of the shed. Dad and Rich were on the job. Then I saw Dad, still in his human form, creep along the side of the little building.

Dad, what are you doing? Stick to the plan! Stick to the . . .

Dad brought something down on the head of the unsuspecting soldier. The man went down like a bag of meal. Dad reached into the man's pockets and emerged with a ring of keys.

"Got them, Rich." I could hear his voice across the quiet compound.

Another shadow emerged from the side of the hut. "Let's get this lock opened," Rich said.

Both of them moved toward the door.

"Dr. Iverson?" JoJo's voice. She was in there.

I started toward them.

"What's going on here?!" The General had stepped out of the elevator and into the afternoon sunshine.

Perfect.

I changed course, charging toward him, squeaking threateningly, even as he drew his gun. Super gopher, on the job! If I could have laughed . . .

I latched onto his pant leg and hung on desperately. Okay, you're in trouble now. You have no idea what I'm capable of.

He looked down and shook me off easily.

Okay. I guess you do. I definitely had to go bigger.

Bear! Now I had his attention.

He tried to level his gun at me, but I knocked it out of his hand with an easy swipe of my paw.

For a moment, we stared at each other. Then I jerked my head toward the other soldiers, still battling the flames at the bottom of the hill.

He just looked at me.

I jerked my head again.

Finally, he caught on. Carefully, he edged past me, then turned and charged down the slope, waving his arms and shouting something unintelligible.

I didn't wait to see the reaction, but made a quick trip to the little hut.

Dad and Rich were still trying keys. "Okay, try the next one," Rich said. Obviously, there were a lot of them.

I shoved my way in and pointed to one key with a claw.

Dad turned, startled, and looked at me.

I grunted and pointed again. The black one. Everything around here opens with the black one!

He separated that key from the bunch and inserted it into the lock. It turned easily and the lock snapped open.

148

Dad swung the door back, revealing JoJo's relieved face. "I am so happy to see you!" she said. She looked at me, hesitating. "I'm assuming you're Todd?!"

I nodded and she threw herself into my arms. "Oh, Todd, I'm so glad to see you! Even furry and . . . huge."

"We'd better get going," Dad said. He thrust a vial into JoJo's hand. "Take this, dear and the rest of us will meet you behind the shed."

JoJo nodded and we left her there.

A moment later, an eagle joined three other eagles, one carrying, of all things, a backpack, and we leapt into the air as one.

The flight to the ranch took much less time than I expected. JoJo, who had flown it several times, knew the currents and navigated them with efficiency.

We circled the familiar buildings once, studying them. Finally, Dad screeched and the rest of us fell into line behind him.

We landed behind Uncle Peter and Aunt Bett's house. The door opened, smacking the side of the house and Uncle Peter appeared in the opening. "Hank? Is that you?"

Dad hopped awkwardly over to his brother, still dragging his backpack.

"It is you!" Peter lifted his head and shouted, "Bett!"

My aunt joined him. "What is it, Hon?" Her eyes got big. "Hank?! Hank!!"

"He's come back!" Uncle Peter said. "Quick! Help me get them into the house!"

The rest of us followed Dad as he hopped through the doorway and disappeared inside.

Chapter Seventeen

"Downstairs," Uncle Peter said, shortly.

Dad nodded.

Uncle Peter went first. Rather than hop, Dad simply opened his wings and let himself glide. Rich, JoJo and I did the same.

"In here!" Uncle Peter said. "Hurry!" He went into the laundry room.

Four eagles trailed along behind him.

By the time I had moved into the little room, things were beginning to get quite crowded. What on earth did he hope of accomplishing by sardine-ing us in here?

Uncle Peter bent over and ran his hand along the base of the wall behind the washing machine.

I heard something click loudly.

Then he stood up again and pushed on one side of the wall. It moved inwards about a foot. "There's not much room to get through, but you'll be comfortable once you're inside," he said.

Dad went first with the rest of us following again. Uncle Peter came through last, pushing the wall shut behind him. Again, I heard a loud click.

We were in absolute darkness.

I was suddenly reminded of my little room back at the ol' military hacienda. It didn't make me the least nostalgic.

"Wait a sec," Uncle Peter's voice came out of the inky blackness. Sounds of movement. Something sliding along the wall.

Suddenly, the room lit up. I looked up. A bare bulb was hanging over our heads. I heaved a sigh of relief. I don't care how safe I am, I still like to be able to see.

We were in a fair-sized room. Nothing had been done to disguise the bare cinder block walls and cement floor.

Obviously, no one stayed here for any length of time. Apparently, this was some sort of storage room.

But why had I never known of its existence?

I glanced around. Shelves on three sides and a large wardrobe on the fourth. Many of the shelves were packed with boxes and cans of food. And some very familiar metal crates. I moved closer.

After the security, such as it was, had been broken in his lab, Dad had moved his equipment into the root cellar. But not the vials of Essence. He had never told me where they had gone. My questions were at last answered.

"You'll probably be changing soon," Uncle Peter said. "I have some boxes of old clothes here on the shelves." He pulled a couple down and set them on the floor. "Help yourselves."

He looked around. "I'm afraid it isn't very comfortable in here, but it's the best we can do until we see what the fallout is from your escape."

A small red light bulb suddenly blinked on near the wall.

"Uh-oh. Someone's coming!" Uncle Peter bent over and released the catch on the wall, then pulled on an almost invisible handle recessed in the cinderblock, opening the 'door'. "I'll be back!" He disappeared through the narrow opening. The wall slid soundlessly shut.

Dad was already over at the box, picking at the contents with his beak. He laid out a couple pairs of pants and a shirt. Then he picked open his backpack and pulled out more clothes.

JoJo hopped over and grabbed a pair of pants and the shirt. Then she hopped over to the corner and, using only her beak, and a lot of wiggling, managed to get her eagle head through the neck of the shirt. Then she faced the wall and waited.

Dad and Rich also grabbed some clothes and parked beside them on the floor. Following JoJo's example, the two of them also faced toward the wall. Obviously, modesty was still to be maintained. My fourteen-year-old self could only feel relief.

A short time later, the three of them had changed, and clothed.

I quickly grabbed the sweatpants I had been wearing earlier in the mine and went to the corner that JoJo had used only moments before.

By the time I had rejoined the rest, Dad had managed to find another shirt and a couple of pairs of old shoes.

I nabbed the shirt.

"Man, how big are your Uncle Peter's feet?" Rich asked as he jammed his own foot into one shoe.

Dad grinned. "Bigger than mine," he said.

"Yeah, it shows."

"Speaking of 'big'," JoJo laughed. She spread out her arms. Her clothes had been left behind at the base and the shirt she was wearing obviously belonged to Uncle Peter. It reached almost to her knees. Fortunately, the oversized pants had a drawstring waist and she was able to cinch them tight enough to keep them on.

Dad was doing a bit better. He had brought the clothes provided by Rich and JoJo in his backpack, so both pants and shirt fit fairly well.

Rich, too, looked pretty good. He was wearing clothes from the backpack as well.

"Huh. This reminds me of when Pete and I grew up," Dad said, continuing to rummage through the box. "I always had to pick through his hand-me-downs." He had finished searching the first box and was going through the second. "Oh. Here are a couple more pairs of shoes," he said. "No. They must be Aunt Bett's. They look pretty small."

JoJo looked at them doubtfully. "Yeah, I don't think those'll fit me, Dr. Iverson."

He threw them back into the box. "I guess that's as good as we can do."

He looked around at JoJo and me in our vastly oversized castoffs and laughed. "Man! You two look like a couple of hoboes!"

"Thanks, Dad." I grinned and wiggled my bare feet.

"Well," he said, "we might be here for a while. I guess we may as well make ourselves as comfortable as possible." He walked over to the shelves and pulled down a crate.

"Here, Rich, take this. We'll need something to sit on."

Rich grabbed the crate and set it on the floor in the center of the room.

Dad handed JoJo and I each a crate. Then he took one for himself.

We settled ourselves in a circle.

He glanced down at our bare feet and frowned. "Won't do to catch a chill off this cold floor," he said finally. "Here. Let's pile some of the other clothes in the middle." He upended both of the boxes, leaving the castoffs in a pile. "Put your feet on those," he directed.

He was right. It did help.

"So, we appear to have some time," he said, settling himself on his crate. "Let's catch up."

"It's chilly in here," JoJo said. "Is there a jacket or anything in the pile?"

"Here's a long-sleeved shirt." I tossed it to her.

"Oh thanks." She pulled it on over the other one. Her head popped out of the neck. "So, where do we start?"

"Well, I'll tell my side, then Todd. Then I want to hear what you two have been up to."

"Good. I've wanted to hear it," JoJo said.

"General Doom . . . er . . . Dune . . ."

"Doom works for me," Rich said.

"Me, too," JoJo added.

"Well, anyway . . ." Dad filled them in.

"I guess you know when I was taken," I said after he had finished.

Both Rich and JoJo nodded. "It was horrible," Rich said. "Jami and I saw them towing the bus into town. The left side was all smashed." He shook his head. "We knew it was your bus, T."

"Yeah." I snorted softly. "It wasn't a picnic being in it, either." I shrugged. "Anyway, I woke up in my little bed at the complex. At first, they let me heal. Then they started feeding me Essence."

Dad rubbed a hand over his face. "I had no idea that they were doing that," he said. "I knew that they were testing it on . . . someone. But I thought, stupidly, that it would be volunteers."

"Yeah," Rich scoffed. "Volunteers in the army!"

"Stupid, I know. I guess I was clinging to hope that some small portion of humanity was still lurking."

"Lurking." I grinned. "Good word."

"So . . .?" JoJo prodded us back to the topic.

"Well, one time I passed out changing back. They panicked and brought Dad."

"That was when I discovered that they had Todd and what they had been doing to him," Dad said. "It wasn't a good day for me."

"Or me, either," I put in. "Shortly after that, I decided I needed to start exploring the complex."

JoJo stared at me. "Ummm . . . T, how did you . . .?"

"Here's the good part, Jo," Rich said, grinning.

"Yes, we now know what happens when one is exposed too many times to Essence, Jo," I said.

"Todd can change at will," Rich grinned.

154

"What?"

I sighed. "It's true, Jo. I can change into any animal whose Essence I've ingested."

Maybe it was just a trick of the light in this dark place, but JoJo seemed to have gone pale.

"Ch-change?" She stumbled over the words.

I nodded. "Yeah. All I have to do is think about an animal. What it was like being that animal. And I can become them."

JoJo's head swivelled toward my dad. "Is this true, Dr. Iverson?"

"I'm afraid so, JoJo," Dad said gently. "It seems to be a permanent side-effect to ingesting too much Essence."

"How do you know when it's too much?"

"Well, I think we can safely say that three times a day, with meals, for three months or so, is too much," I said.

"Got it," Rich grinned at me. "So there *was* a bear!"

I nodded, feeling rather sheepish.

"Well, personally, I think it's cool!" Rich said.

"I will, too," Dad said, looking at me. "After a few years and tests, prove that it hasn't damaged my son.

"I think I agree with that," JoJo said softly.

"Well, I guess we'll never know if it did any mental damage," Rich said.

Ha-ha. Thanks, Rich.

"So you explored the complex?" JoJo said.

"Yeah. I'd escape as a fly . . ."

"A fly!"

Dad cleared his throat. "We've made a few . . . changes to the Essence that you know and love, JoJo."

"I would say so. A fly! I had no idea you could go so small."

"Well, it's just a matter of manipulating the air space," Dad said.

155

JoJo nodded. "I guess it shouldn't be a surprise to me. But it is."

Dad nodded. "I really didn't think it would be successful." He slapped me on the back. "But Todd is here to prove to us that it is."

"Yeah. Actually, it was the worst to get used to," I said. "In fact, that was what I was changing from when I passed out."

"A bit scary for the both of us," Dad said.

"Wow. A fly!" Rich said.

JoJo grinned. "Look who just caught up."

"So back to my story. I would go somewhere quiet and change into a dog. Then I wandered the complex, getting the floor plan fixed in my head. That sort of thing."

"And he managed to overhear quite a bit of important information," Dad said.

"Yeah, for one thing, I know that Dad and I had become a liability and that the rest of the officers were pressing Doom to make a decision about us."

"Liability?' JoJo squeaked.

I nodded. "Not an easy thing to hear. But it sure put a fire under us to get our situation sorted out."

"It wasn't long after that when the alarm went off. The rest you know."

Rich and JoJo were silent for a minute.

"Wow," Rich said, finally.

"So now tell us your side," Dad said to JoJo.

"Well, it's not as exciting as yours," she began, "but it does start after Todd's bus accident."

"Yeah, that was pretty exciting," Rich put in.

I made a face at him.

"Rich and Jami and I figured that the two attempts on Todd were probably Doom trying to scare you into thinking that your lives were in danger."

"Rich told us that," Dad said. "You're probably right."

156

"Anyway, it turns out that Jami's dad is a retired Major from the JTF," JoJo said, "but one who has kept up a lot of his contacts."

"Rich sort of told us that, as well," I said.

"Geeze, Rich, can't you leave any of the story to me?"

Rich grinned. "I guess not, Jo."

"Jami found out that there was a military presence in the Sweetgrass Hills and I spent some time over there until I found the installation."

"Yeah. Took her all of an hour," Rich said.

"Well, it was really quite easy, once I had a general idea of where to look. I mean, it's sorta hard to hide tire tracks on a dirt road."

"I see your point," Dad said.

"Anyway, once Rich and I had narrowed down the location, all we had to do was study things a bit to come up with some possible solutions."

"That's when JoJo decided to build that nest."

"We figured that at least it would interrupt schedules enough that we could sort of get an idea of what to do next. It succeeded past all of our hopes."

"Yeah. I couldn't believe it when they actually marched you out of the place and locked you in the shed," Rich said.

"I was waiting out of sight, but holding a vial of essence for a quick getaway," JoJo said.

"And I was the go-between," Rich added.

"I wrote the note to you and Rich delivered it." JoJo grinned. "That was really quick thinking on your part to direct us to the lab."

"It was all I could think of," I said. "I chose Monday because my room was guarded by a slacker who tended to party all weekend and take Mondays off. It was our best shot at getting away undetected."

157

I rolled my eyes. "But, things didn't work out quite the way we planned them."

Dad looked at me.

Oh, yeah. He hadn't heard this part, either.

"I was wondering what took you so long to get to the lab," Dad said. "You had some problems?"

"A few. Doom decided to join me for breakfast, first."

"Oh, no!"

"Oh, yes! I went into the bathroom and then followed him out the door. Barely. Then I changed into a dog, as I had been doing, and got caught."

"Todd!"

"It gets better. The soldiers dragged the dog to the kennel, collared and tied him and locked him in."

"Okay, your lengthy arrival time is getting better understood," Dad said. "Now, I'm wondering how you got there at all."

"Well, I was able to change into my fly self again and find a vent. From there, I discovered that, though I could get into the vent, I couldn't make any headway against the air flow, so I became a racoon. Then I found the vent into the hall, changed back into a fly, flew to your lab and let myself in."

"Whew!" Dad shook his head.

"That's when you came out through the window," Rich said. "Huh. You know, I thought I saw a coyote standing beside you, Dr. Iverson. For a second, I wondered why you had asked for Essence when you obviously had access to it there."

"We didn't. They kept it all locked up," I said.

Rich nodded. "But then I figured I had imagined it and forgot about it in the excitement of getting away."

"They sent two panthers after you," JoJo said.

158

"We . . . ummm . . . saw them," Dad said. "Just after I took a header down the hill."

"Yeah. We had a bit of an altercation," I said.

Rich laughed. "Yeah. An altercation."

JoJo frowned at us.

I sighed. "We discovered that becoming an animal doesn't necessarily equip you to fight as that animal," I said. I looked at Rich. "Although Rich did okay."

"Yeah, well, I've had a bit more practice than the rest of you."

"Oh, yeah, I keep forgetting about your bank-robbing days," JoJo said, batting him in the arm.

Rich grimaced and rubbed his arm. "I wish I could forget it," he said slowly. Rich had been forced to steal Essence and use it to help his two uncles rob banks. Not a happy time for him.

"Anyway," I said, "between us coyotes and the cougar, we managed to fight the cats off. They were re-grouping when we saw the eagle go for them."

"Yes, well, Rich and I decided that I should wait out of sight, but with Essence ready just like before. Then, if anyone followed you, I should try to stop them, or at least harass and confuse them so they lost your trail." She grimaced. "It sort of worked."

"Yeah. We saw you dive. Then we heard the cats protesting."

"It didn't take much to discourage them from following you," JoJo said. "They were pretty protective of their eyes."

She frowned. "Unfortunately, it didn't occur to me that I should be on the watch for anything threatening me."

I caught my breath. "What happened, Jo?"

"Some joker with a bow and arrow winged me." She pushed up the sleeve of her shirt, showing us a slender, pink mark. "The arrow ran across my wing, just here above the joint. I dropped like a stone."

For a moment, I felt faint. JoJo threatened? JoJo in danger?

Again, I saw a familiar red haze.

She reached out her hand and clasped mine. "It's all right, T," she said softly. She lifted her head and went on. "I didn't have far to fall. Mostly, it only knocked the breath out of me."

"The soldier with the bow scooped me up and carried me into the building." She frowned. "I must have passed out because I don't remember much else until I woke up in a small, brightly-lighted room.

"Someone had wrapped a towel or blanket around me, imprisoning one wing against my body and leaving the injured one out and another soldier, a woman, was looking at the wound."

"Must have been the lieutenant who was everlastingly trying to look after me," I said.

"Well, a woman at any rate." She narrowed her eyes. "Come to think of it, it did say 'lieutenant' on her name tag."

"They wore name tags?" I said.

JoJo looked at me. "How long did you say they had you locked up?"

I grinned sheepishly and shrugged. "I just never noticed."

"T, remind me not to recommend you for the next top spy."

"Agreed."

"I changed shortly after that and told her not to bother trying to stitch the gash, but just to put a bandage over it. It would heal soon enough on its own.

"She looked surprised, but didn't argue with me and did what I asked."

"So now they know how well we can heal," Dad said softly.

"I'm afraid so, Dr. Iverson," JoJo said.

He sighed. "Well, it can't be helped. At least you are all right."

"They put me in a room with a TV and some gaming systems, so I wasn't too bored," JoJo said.

"Hey! That must have been my room!" I said, excitedly.

"I wondered."

"Did they take good care of you?" Dad asked.

"Well, the first little while, the lieutenant kept checking on me, but, after she could see that my wound had all but healed, she left me alone."

"They had just served me supper when the alarm went off."

She frowned suddenly.

"What's the matter?" I asked her.

"I just realized I didn't get to eat anything."

"You must be starving!" Dad said. He got to his feet and began to poke around the shelves. "Let's see what we can find."

He emerged with several cans of fruit and some boxes of crackers. "Here. We can start with these," he said. "There's also some beef jerky and some bags of chips."

"Oh this looks good, Dr. I," JoJo said, twisting the lid off a bottle of peaches and tearing off the inside seal.

For several minutes, the four of us slurped up fruit and crunched our way through several packets of crackers.

"Well, I think I can guess what happened next in your tale, JoJo," Dad said, finally.

JoJo wiped her mouth on her shirt and smiled. "Two of them hauled me out of the complex and pushed me into that little shed," she said. "I was actually surprised. I didn't think they'd do the same thing that they had done with Todd."

"They probably didn't realize that Todd made contact with us while he was incarcerated in the shed," Dad said. "For all they knew, our plan was carried out by the two of us."

"I guess," I nodded. "They might think that you managed to get your hands on some Essence. Smuggle it in to me and the two of us made our escape."

"Unless they happened to notice that you were fighting alongside a cougar," Rich pointed out.

"And didn't attach any importance to the girl/eagle who flew to your rescue," JoJo added.

"Or the bear," Rich said.

"You're right," I said. "That reminds me of something. When the cougar first contacted me, I thought it was you, Jo."

"But I'm always the cougar," Rich said.

"Yeah. But for some reason, I thought Jo was the cougar and Rich, the eagle."

"Didn't you notice that the eagle was female, son?" Dad asked.

I frowned. "Again, my powers of observation are called into question."

"And sneered at," Rich laughed.

"Okay, so I didn't notice."

"And that the cougar was most definitely male," Dad grinned.

Rich turned a lively shade of red.

"I didn't notice that, either."

Dad shook his head. "Todd, I sometimes wonder why we keep you around."

JoJo laughed at that. "It's because he's so sweet, Dr. I," she said. "We've been through this before." She leaned forward and kissed my cheek.

162

My face went as red as Rich's.

Dad and JoJo laughed.

"Actually, we wouldn't have escaped if it weren't for you, Todd," Rich had recovered his voice.

I looked at him.

"Really. When Doom came out of the complex and pulled his gun, I thought we were done."

"Yes, son, that was quick thinking with the bear."

"Oh, yeah." I had forgotten about that. "Actually, I didn't even think. I just reacted. I tried to attack as a gopher, but you can just guess how that worked out. All I could think was 'bigger. I must go bigger'."

"Well it worked out perfectly. As though it had been planned."

Suddenly, we heard a noise. A heavy click.

Dad stood up and herded the rest of us back against the far wall.

Uncle Peter poked his head in. "All clear for the moment," he said. He glanced down at the empty fruit containers and assorted rubbish left over from our impromptu meal. "I guess I don't have to offer you any supper!"

Chapter Eighteen

We climbed the stairs behind my uncle.

"Oh, Hank! Todd! I'm so glad to see you!" Aunt Bett met us at the top of the stairs and wrapped me in a tearful hug.

"It's good to be back, sis," Dad said, patting her arm.

"Come in. Come in. I've got supper all prepared!" She steered us into the dining room. "Now. Tell me all about it!"

* * *

"Do you think we dare go home?" Dad was talking to Uncle Peter.

"I don't Bro," he said. "The military had the whole crew out here this afternoon while you were locked in the storage room. They are keeping a pretty watchful eye on your place." He grinned, "Not quite so watchful an eye on this place, though, fortunately."

"They never discovered that storage room, though they did a pretty thorough search of this house and the ranch after you first disappeared." He shrugged. "I think they finally decided that you must have moved your stock of Essence off the property."

"So what can we do?"

"Well, Bett can get Rich and JoJo home," Uncle Peter said. "We'll just have to change them into something small."

"That's right! I never even thought about your families!" Dad said. "They must be worried sick about you!"

"I called them just after you arrived," Uncle Peter said. He looked at Rich and JoJo and grinned.

"Yes, Peter told them, rather cryptically I might add . . ." Aunt Bett turned and smiled at her husband, " . . . that he had picked up JoJo and Rich so they could help him out. I don't think their families minded."

"We still aren't sure that these phone lines are clear," Uncle Peter put in.

Dad snorted. "Like the days of the party lines."

Uncle Peter grinned. "Remember how we got messages through when Old Man Ramsay was still on our line?"

"Yeah. Kinda fun!" Dad said.

"Anyway, I didn't dare say too much for fear of . . . saying too much."

"Their families were fine with it," Aunt Bett said. "But they did ask when you two would be back."

"Us two?" I asked. "You mean Dad and me?"

She nodded.

"Are you telling me that no one knew we had been kidnapped?" I said.

"I don't know who started the story, but someone told the school principal that your dad had left for a while to do some research and that he had taken you with him."

"Huh. Jerks."

"Todd!"

"Well, they are." I was unrepentant.

"Someone else has been pretty persistent about finding out about you as well," Bett said.

Dad looked at her. "Oh? Who?"

"That cute little Dr. Linden," Aunt Bett grinned.

Dad . . . blushed. I stared at him.

Aunt Bett laughed. "Anyway, she has been calling almost daily to find out if we've heard anything about you."

"You didn't tell her anything?"

"Hank, we didn't know anything," Uncle Peter said.

"All we knew was that you had disappeared," Aunt Bett said. "Then that General Whoosis tried to tell us that you were in protective custody."

"Is that what he said?"

"Yeah. We didn't really know if we should believe him," Uncle Peter said.

Dad snorted. "Well, we were in his custody. And that's what they kept telling us too."

"Yeah," I put in, "that we were there for our protection."

"Anyway, we were pretty much going crazy with worry when JoJo and Rich contacted us," Uncle Peter said.

"It was so nice to have something proactive to do," Aunt Bett said.

"Yeah, at least we could dole out Essence and hope that some good might come of it," Uncle Peter said.

"Well, it made all the difference," JoJo said. "Without your help, we never would have been able to find these two, let alone get them out of there."

Uncle Peter stood up and stretched. "Well, at least you're back home now," he said. He turned and looked at Rich and JoJo. "We'd better get these two on their way."

"Can't we just stay here with you?" JoJo asked, clutching my arm. "You were gone for such a long time . . ."

Dad smiled. "I'm afraid not, JoJo," he said, getting to his feet.

She sighed.

"Come on. Let's see what we can do with you," he said.

JoJo turned to me. "Will you be at school tomorrow?"

"I really don't know, Jo," I told her. "That all depends on how safe Dad thinks it is."

"I really doubt it, JoJo," Dad said softly. "Sorry."

166

She slumped. "I guess I'm ready, then." Rich and JoJo followed Dad into the basement.

"Better let them have some privacy, Todd," Uncle Peter said when I started to follow.

"Privacy? After all we've been through?"

He laughed. "I guess you have a point."

I reached the small room, just as Dad handed each of them a vial.

"Well, I guess it was just a matter of time before I tried something different," Rich said, breaking the top off his vial.

"I still prefer something a little closer to the top of the food chain," JoJo said, grimacing.

Both of them disappeared.

Dad gently probed the two piles of discarded clothing.

When he stood up, he was holding two small, grey mice.

I reached out a hand and one of them scrambled onto my palm.

"Jo?"

It nodded.

I sighed. "Sorry about all of this."

The mouse sneezed and blinked black eyes at me.

"Shall we go?"

I followed Dad up the stairs.

Aunt Bett was standing at the door. "Here, guys," she said. She held open the oversized pockets of her coat. "You'll be safe here."

"Hmmm . . . maybe not," Dad said.

She turned to look at him. "You have a better idea?"

"Well, I'm just thinking about what might happen if you got stopped."

"Oh. That may be a problem," Bett agreed. "What do you suggest?"

167

Dad looked thoughtful. "Hmmm." He frowned.

"Maybe it would be better if we just let them roam around inside the car," Uncle Peter said.

"You're probably right," Dad said. "That way, they can hide if they need to."

"I don't like the idea of them not being strapped in," Aunt Bett said.

"Well, you'll just have to make sure you don't have an accident," Dad grinned.

Aunt Bett punched him in the arm. Again, she held her pockets open. "Well, let's get you out to the car at least."

I dropped JoJo into one pocket and Dad put Rich into the other. "Have a safe trip, you two," he said.

"Yeah. Please," I added.

JoJo poked her head out of the pocket and looked at me. Then she disappeared.

"I'll see you really soon, Jo," I whispered.

"Okay, I'll be right back," Bett said.

Just then, the doorbell pealed.

We all looked at each other.

"Now who can that be?" Bett said.

"Quick, Todd, Hank! Down to the room!" Uncle Peter herded us toward the stairs.

I dove down them with Dad on my heels.

"Oh, hello, private," Aunt Bett's voice reached us faintly. "What can I do for you?"

Uncle Peter closed the hidden door.

An hour later, he was back.

"You guys all right?"

"We're going to have to install a few conveniences if Todd and I are going to have to keep hiding here," Dad said wearily, getting stiffly to his feet.

"Yeah. Like a bathroom," I said, charging up the stairs. I rejoined them a few minutes later in the front room.

Aunt Bett was standing near the window, peeking out through one of the drapes.

Dad and Uncle Peter were sitting on the couch.

"Aunt Bett!" I dropped into a chair. "Did everything go well?"

She turned away from the window and made a face. "Pretty well," she said.

"You'd better start at the beginning," Dad said.

"I'm all ears," I said.

She smiled. "Todd, you're so like your dad!"

I glanced at my father. "No one else I'd rather be compared to, Aunt Bett."

She laughed. "When you guys were hot-footing it for the basement, I was talking to a young private who had been assigned here for the first time." She grimaced again. "Apparently his instructions weren't too extensive. He was under the impression that he was guarding us."

I raised an eyebrow.

"Guarding us?" Dad seemed equally surprised.

"Yeah. He asked if there was anything he could do to make us more comfortable. Then he reassured me that he and his buddies would keep us safe."

"That doesn't sound right." I stared at her.

"Well, that's what he said."

Dad turned to Uncle Peter. "What did the soldiers say who were here earlier?"

Uncle Peter blinked. "Ummm . . . let me think." He frowned. "They said they were looking for you."

"And that's all?"

His brow furrowed thoughtfully. "I think so . . ." His face cleared. "No, wait! They also said that it was important that they find you and that we tell them anything we might find out. I just assumed that they were looking for you to try to lock you up again,"

"As did I," Dad said.

"I wonder if it's a bit more complicated than that?"

Dad frowned. Then he shook his head. "Let's not get ahead of ourselves," he said. "We know that they will lock us up if they find us."

"However they are trying to justify themselves," I added.

Dad nodded. "Whatever their reasons, Todd and I don't want to go back there."

"Definitely agree," Aunt Bett said.

"So what are our alternatives?"

"Well, you can stay in our basement," Uncle Peter said.

Dad made a face.

"Well, let's not think about it tonight," Aunt Bett got to her feet.

I stood up with her. "But you didn't tell us about your trip into town. With JoJo," I said.

"Oh. Right." She took a deep breath and sat down again.

I dropped back into my seat.

"Well, I made it out to the car. The young soldier walked with me and even opened my door. That was a bit . . . scary."

I nodded. "Go on."

"He told me to drive safely and pushed the car door shut. Then he gave me a bit of a salute and turned away. That was when I told Rich and JoJo to find a place to hide. Both of them scrambled out of my pockets and disappeared. I started into town." She shook her head. "I hadn't gone very far when I realized that there was a car following me."

"Bett!" Uncle Peter looked shocked.

"Yes. Well, as it turned out, they didn't try to stop me or anything, but I can tell you, I was pretty worried while I tried to figure out how to drop those two kids off without arousing any attention."

"What did you do?"

"I went to the convenience store and bought a few groceries. Then I asked them to deliver them to JoJo's house."

"Bett, that's genius!" Dad grinned.

"Well, I hope it worked out all right. I know that they had some time before they changed, but not much."

The phone rang.

We all stared at it.

"Maybe that's them!" I said, leaping up.

"Careful, Todd, it might be tapped," Uncle Peter said. "Better let me answer it." He walked calmly to the phone and picked it up. "Hello?"

He listened for a moment. "Okay. Thank you!" He hung up.

"Was it . . .?" I jiggled his elbow.

"That was JoJo's mother," Uncle Peter said, smiling and gently pulling his arm from my grip. "She sounded a bit confused. Said something about some groceries."

"Oh, good. She got them," Aunt Bett said.

"She also said that JoJo wanted us to know that she got her homework done."

Relief.

Aunt Bett smiled. "I guess that mysterious message means that everything has been taken care of," she said.

"I guess so," Dad said doubtfully.

"Of course it does," I told them. "It makes perfect sense."

"Well, I'm glad you speak 'JoJo'," Dad grinned.

Uncle Peter looked at me. "I'd say he was getting pretty fluent," he said.

I felt my face grow hot.

"See?"

They all laughed.

"So. Anywhere we can sleep?" I asked.

"Of course, dear," Aunt Bett said.

"I think you'd better take the bed in the basement room, so you can scramble if you need to," Uncle Peter added.

"Thanks, Bro, Sis," Dad said. "Sorry about all of this."

"Like any of it was your fault, Hank," Bett said, rising up on her toes and giving Dad a kiss on the cheek.

He grinned. "Well, I'm sorry anyway."

Chapter Nineteen

I looked down.

There was an army jeep parked just at the ranch entrance. Several soldiers were patrolling on foot nearby.

I flew east.

Along the bluff, several more soldiers were stationed, each with a careful eye, and rifle, trained on the ranch buildings across the river. South and west told the same story.

A small group showed briefly as they patrolled the long, tree-lined drive.

We were virtually in lock-down.

I sighed and let myself drift toward Uncle Peter's house.

* * *

Dad was going through his backpack. "So there's no way to get out?"

"None that I could see, Dad."

He rubbed his chin. "What to do . . .?"

I peered over his shoulder. "What are you doing?"

He looked down at the papers in his hands. "Going over the notes I managed to smuggle out of the lab."

I sat down. "Really? You got your information out?"

"Well, some of it." Dad grinned. "A coyote or eagle on the run can only carry so much!"

"True."

"I think we need to get to Ms. Scott's boss," Uncle Peter said, leaning back in his chair and propping his stockinged feet up on the coffee table.

Dad looked at him and nodded. "I agree," he said. "I may not like the guy, but he knows the situation and will probably be our best bet for getting out of it."

I vaguely remembered him. "Was he the little porky guy who came out with Ms. Scott once?"

"Actually, twice," Dad said, "but I don't think you were around the second time. And yes, that's the guy."

"Didn't he leave you his card?" I had an equally hazy memory of seeing Dad with one in his hand.

"Yeah, he did," Dad said. "But it's over there," he jerked his head in the direction of our house, "with everything else we own."

"Maybe I can get in and get it," I suggested. I pictured a bug. A fly.

"And carry it how?"

I slumped back in my chair. "Right."

"Anyway, I think I remember basically where his office was in Lethbridge," Dad said. "I think our best bet is to try to get there."

"Well, that shouldn't be too hard," Uncle Peter said. "We'll just shrink you down and take you with Bett and me on our next trip."

"Yes," Bett spoke up. "We've pretty well set up Thursdays as our regular Lethbridge day, so leaving then won't be examined too closely."

"We hope," Uncle Peter grinned.

"So. Three days." Dad said. He sighed. "I guess we can wait until then."

"Unless you think we could risk it sooner," Uncle Peter said.

Dad shook his head. "They're obviously on high alert now. They just might take it into their heads to search any vehicle leaving the ranch."

Uncle Peter nodded. "So, Thursday, it is."

* * *

The doorbell pealed at dawn the following morning.

Uncle Peter looked up from his orange juice. "What now?" He got to his feet and looked at us, but Dad and I were already on our way downstairs.

A short time later, he joined us in the storage room. "False alarm," he said. "Just that helpful young private telling us he was back on duty and wondering if there was anything we needed."

"He sure seems to be different from the rest of the soldiers," Dad said.

"Yeah. No one else seems to take the same personal interest in us that he does."

"Must come from a nice family."

Uncle Peter laughed. "I was thinking the same thing myself," he said. "That kid must have been taught well."

Dad smiled. "Well, I would like to finish my breakfast."

"And I'm going out on another patrol." I said.

"Careful, son," Dad said.

I grinned at him. "Always, Dad."

* * *

It had gotten quite cloudy and the temperature had dropped. I had a hard time finding a thermal to give me some height. I struggled upwards under my own wing power.

This was almost like work.

Finally, I was high enough to get a good view of the entire ranch.

There were still several groups of soldiers patrolling the perimeters and making their way carefully across the ranch itself. But this time, something was different. One group had gathered in the barnyard.

As I watched, they dropped three white squares down in a semi-circle. Then someone placed a fourth opposite the

175

middle square. Huh. Someone was staging an impromptu baseball game.

I heard the crack of a ball against a bat and a runner scampered toward first base amidst the cheers from his teammates. Nice to know they were human.

I moved on.

Suddenly, something whizzed past me. I turned my head. It was too small and going too fast to be a baseball . . .

Another one. Bullets! Someone was shooting at me!

I banked frantically to one side, then started following an erratic course toward the nearest shelter. The barn.

Several more bullets shot past, one breaking a couple of my tail feathers. I banked heavily again and continued my erratic course.

I dove under the shelter at the back of the barn and leaped up through one of the hay chutes and into the hay loft.

"He's in the barn!" someone shouted. I heard the door smack against the wall and booted feet charge toward the hayloft stairs.

I dropped into the nearest pile of hay and pictured a mouse.

"Block the chutes!" Several people entered the room and fanned out.

I peered out through a screen of hay.

"I don't see an eagle, sir," one of them said, softly, his eyes frantically surveying the rafters over their heads.

"He's here," another voice said. "I saw him come in here."

I beat a hasty retreat under the hay, toward the wall, then found a crack to weasel into and held my breath.

"Be careful," the second voice spoke again. "He's probably hiding under the hay. Don't step on him."

"Yes, sir."

Hmm. Nice to know they were so concerned with my welfare. Just minutes after they had tried to shoot me out of the sky with a high-powered rifle.

For several minutes, the heavy footsteps crossed and re-crossed the loft. Soldiers gingerly poked piles of hay and straw.

One of them spoke up. "Sir, we don't even know if it was one of them."

Silence.

Another, "He's right, sir. It could have been a real eagle."

Someone snickered. "We must have scared the tail feathers off him!"

Laughter.

Sometime later, someone sighed. "He must have dived out right after he dove in."

"Yes, sir."

"C'mon, men, this is a lost cause."

"Doom's not going to be pleased."

"Dune, soldier and don't you forget it!"

Meekly, "Yes, sir. Excuse me, sir."

"Let's go, men." Footsteps pounding down the stairs.

I waited until the sounds of their passage had faded, then I crawled out of the hole and nosed my way through the straw. Finally, reaching a cleared spot, I changed into a cat.

There was a scramble of feet. "Holy Geeze!" someone said.

I looked up.

A soldier who had been seated on a bale beside the stairway was staring at me.

Wonderful.

He scrambled, belatedly, for his side arm, screaming for his commanding officer.

I didn't wait to see who would answer, but dove back into the straw and thought of the smallest thing I could.

Finally, a beetle scurried across the floor and up the nearest wall. Sigh. Well, at least I could see.

This time, the soldiers were even more thorough in their search. All of the straw was scraped together and sifted carefully. Then the bales were moved, one at a time and stacked neatly.

I watched all of their industry with a smug, bug smile on my face. They'd never find me. I glanced around. But never, in the history of this ranch, had this hay loft been so scrupulously clean.

Finally, there was simply nowhere else to look, except for the cracks in the walls.

Again, my smile.

The exhausted soldiers slumped against the walls, their equally tired commander in their midst.

"What now, sir?"

"Hanged if I know," he said. "We've searched everywhere." He turned to look at the hay chutes. Five in all. He walked over to one and peered down through it.

"Soldier?"

"Right here, sir."

"See anything?"

"Nothing has come through here, sir."

"Everyone sound off!"

"Nothing here, sir!" another voice said, a bit further away.

"All clear!"

"All clear!"

"All clear!"

"Damn!" He walked over to the stairway. "Well, this is a total waste of time. It obviously must have gotten out, somehow."

"In my opinion, sir, the eagle never actually entered the barn and Grimm just caught sight of an old tom cat."

"But I saw it change!" another soldier protested.

"Right," someone else said.

"I did! A small, grey mouse came out of the hay and changed into a cat."

"So now mice can change into cats?"

"It did! I saw it!"

"Leave it, Grimm. Tompkins."

"Yes, sir."

"Sorry, sir."

He sighed. "Well, we're not doing much good here. Let's go, men."

Again, they trooped down the stairs.

This time, I cautiously made my way along the wall and peered carefully down through the hay chute below me. A few seconds later, a sparrow flew out from beneath the shed and headed toward Uncle Peter's.

* * *

"At least they're alert," Uncle Peter said.

Dad made a face. "Yeah. Too alert," he said glumly.

"Oh, c'mon, Bro! If there really are bad guys out there, it's nice to know that they can't get in here. With us."

Dad made a face. "I'd feel a lot better if we actually knew they were guarding us and not just trying to catch us."

Uncle Peter nodded. "I guess there is that," he said. "Well, tomorrow is the big day. Then, if all goes well, you won't have to worry any more."

"Yeah. 'Cause things have been going so well for us this far," I said.

"You're so right, son," Dad agreed.

"Well, we'd better get some sleep," Uncle Peter said, getting to his feet. "One way or the other, it's going to be a big day tomorrow."

Chapter Twenty

"Okay, we're coming to the gate," Uncle Peter whispered. "Keep your heads down."

Dad and I climbed up inside the rear seat of the truck and curled up in a spring.

Now here's something to tell my grandkids, I thought.

Dad looked at me and nodded.

The truck slowed.

"Okay, it looks as though they are going to let us . . . no! Wait! They're pulling us over."

"Peter!"

"It'll be okay, Bett," he said, soothingly.

"Hmm . . ."

The truck stopped and I could hear the squeak as Uncle Peter rolled down his window. "Anything I can do for you, private?"

"Not at all," someone said through the window. "Just wanted to see if everything was going okay with you."

"We're fine," Uncle Peter said. "Just feeling a bit lonely today."

"Lonely?"

"Yeah. My husband is missing his brother," Bett said. "You can't blame him. They've been together all their lives. It's a habit that's a bit hard to break."

"Ah, yes. I see."

"You have a brother?" Uncle Peter asked.

"No. Three sisters, though."

"Miss them?"

"Oddly enough, I do. At times."

"Well, I'm missing my brother and I was wondering if you could tell me when he would be able to return to the ranch."

"Return?" The private was obviously drawing a blank. "Ummm . . . here?"

Uncle Peter snorted softly. "Of course here," he said. "Where else would he go?"

"Sorry, sir. Of course, sir."

"Now if you don't mind, Bett and I have our errands to run and we have a long trip ahead of us."

"Of course, sir. Sorry to have detained you."

More squeaking as Uncle Peter rolled up his window. Then he put the truck in gear.

"Upstart!" he mumbled.

"What, dear?"

"Nothing." He stepped on the gas.

* * *

Thursdays usually aren't very remarkable in Lethbridge. Sort of like every other day of the week.

This one was no exception.

"So where do you want to start?" Uncle Peter asked, moving slowly north along Mayor Magrath Drive.

"Just let me get my shirt on and I'll tell you," Dad said, his voice muffled. "Okay." His head popped out. "I think the address was somewhere on Fifth Avenue North. I remember thinking it must be somewhere near the Christian Elementary school there."

"Oh, yeah. I know where that is." Uncle Peter signalled and made a turn.

* * *

"So what do you think?"

Uncle Peter had pulled the truck over to the curb.

I glanced out the window. Directly across from us was a small school. I twisted around and looked the other way. A house. Or what passed for a house. "Do you really think this might be the place?"

182

Dad frowned. "It certainly doesn't look like it," he said doubtfully.

"Yeah, well, that would make it perfect!" Uncle Peter grinned. He let go of the wheel and dropped his hands into his lap. "So, do you want us to come with you?"

Dad looked thoughtful. "Probably not, Bro," he said, finally. "Better not to put all of our eggs in one basket."

"Yeah. In case we get broken. Or scrambled," Uncle Peter said, grinning.

Great, a chicken metaphor. My favourite kind. Not.

Uncle Peter opened the door and slid out. "Well, you're the boss," he said, flipping the switch and pulling his seat forward.

"Yeah, and don't you forget it!" Dad grinned, crawling out.

I followed him.

"Do you think Todd should go with you?" Aunt Bett looked worried.

"Todd is the one who can convince them that we are telling the truth," Dad said. "I don't like it but . . . well, there you go."

Uncle Peter nodded. "They'll be fine, hon," he said.

Aunt Bett nodded, but still looked doubtful.

"We'll be right back," Dad said.

The two of us walked up to the door and pushed the bell. "Shouldn't we be looking for a phone booth or something?" I asked.

Dad looked at me. "A phone booth?"

"Yeah. Like in 'Get Smart'. He always gets in via a phone booth."

Dad laughed. "Right. Tell you what. You look around for a phone booth and I'll talk to the enemy agent who answers this door." Dad knocked.

An elderly man opened the door. "What can I do for you folks?"

"Oh, I'm looking for someone named . . ." Dad frowned, thoughtfully, " . . . umm . . ." He looked at me. "I've just drawn a blank!"

I laughed. "Dad has no memory for names," I said quickly. "I think the person we're looking for is a man named Whitaker."

"Ah. Whitaker!" the old man nodded. "Yes." He looked over Dad's shoulder toward the street. "You're best bet would be to go to that phone booth over there and look through the book."

Dad spun around and stared.

I did the same. A phone booth? "You're kidding, right?"

He looked at me. "Not that I'm aware of," he said quietly. He nodded toward the booth again. "Go ahead. Try it." He closed the door.

Dad and I looked at each other. "This is by far the weirdest thing I've ever done," he said, finally. He stepped back and waved at Uncle Peter, then pointed toward the phone booth. Uncle Peter waved and smiled. I could hear CCR's 'Bad Moon Rising' playing on the truck's radio.

Was that an omen?

Dad and I walked over to the phone booth. It looked normal enough. I pushed the door open. It rolled smoothly. Soundlessly.

Dad stepped inside and I squeezed in behind him and pushed the door shut.

"Now what?"

"Now we look through the phonebook, I guess." Dad flipped through a dog-eared book. "Here!" he pointed. "Whitaker!"

I peered past him. "There are three of them."

"Yeah, but I'm pretty sure his first name started with a 'J'."

"Huh. The only 'J' Whitaker here is Jonas P."

"That must be our man. Dad dropped a quarter into the phone and dialled. The phone clicked loudly.

Then the floor dropped out from under us.

* * *

"Ouch!"

"Are you okay, son?"

"Yeah. I just banged my elbow on something." I struggled to my feet.

We hadn't fallen far. Only a few feet. Dad was already standing, looking around.

We were in a round, cement room, about eight feet high, about twice that wide, and smooth walled and windowless. Several fluorescent fixtures in the ceiling provided light.

"Well. I really didn't expect to see the two of you!" a voice said.

We both spun around. A door, concealed perfectly in the smooth walls, had opened silently. Ms. Scott's boss was framed in the gap.

"Ah, Whitaker!" Dad moved toward him. "Just the man I want to see."

"How do you do, Dr. Iverson," Whitaker said. He glanced around and grinned. "Welcome to my . . . office!" Then he stepped back. "Won't you and your son come with me?"

Dad glanced at me and shrugged. Then he followed the short, round man through the doorway.

I followed Dad. We were in a long corridor, leading away from the entry.

"Let's just duck in here, shall we?" Whitaker pushed at a door about halfway down the hallway. It swung open, revealing a small room with a table and a couple of chairs. He reached inside and flipped a switch. Then he stepped back and allowed Dad and I to precede him. He followed us and pushed the door shut. "Please take a seat."

Dad pushed a chair toward me and took the other.

Whitaker put soft, pudgy hands on the table and leaned toward us. "So, am I to guess that you have reconsidered my offer, Dr. Iverson?"

"Umm . . . no, Whitaker," Dad said. "Actually, we are here to file a report and to ask for your help."

He raised his eyebrows. "My help?"

"Yes." Dad cleared his throat. "Now what I am about to tell you may seem a bit . . . far-fetched, but please hear me out."

Whitaker moved to the side of the table and leaned a hip on it. "I'm ready, Dr. Iverson."

Dad glanced at me. "We . . . that is, Todd and I . . . have been the 'guests' of the military for the past couple of months."

"Military?" Whitaker's eyes narrowed. "Where?"

Dad paused. "We were smuggled in and smuggled out," he said, finally. "I . . . I really don't know where."

I looked at him, frowning. He knew! We all knew!

Dad kept his eyes on Whitaker.

"So how did you escape?"

"Some . . . friends helped us," Dad said.

"Ah. Nice to have friends like that."

Dad smiled. "It really is."

"So," Whitaker looked at his fingernails, "what do you need from me?"

Again, Dad hesitated. "We want to be able to go home," he said at last. "I want Todd to be able to go back to school and not worry that he's going to be picked up and deposited back in his prison cell."

"Prison cell? I thought you said you were being held by the military."

"There are all kinds of prison cells, Whitaker," Dad said, quietly.

"You're so right, Dr. Iverson," the short man said. He laughed. "Actually, I'm glad you came to me," he said, sliding off the table. "This makes things amazingly easier." He opened the door.

Two men stood there, dressed in black and holding rifles.

Chapter Twenty One

"Now, if you will be so kind as to accompany me and my friends . . ."

Dad stayed where he was and looked at Whitaker. "It was you. All this time, it was you."

"You've proved to be rather slippery to get hold of," Whitaker said, beckoning to the two men in black.

They stepped into the room.

He turned back to us. "The people I represent weren't any too pleased when you disappeared. I must say it was rather rude of you, when we had gone to such lengths to capture you."

"The bus? The dressing room?"

"I admit the attempts weren't very sophisticated." Whitaker laughed. "But then, we didn't think they really needed to be. After all, we were dealing with country people."

"So what you're saying is that people from the country are just a bit behind you lucky dogs from the great metropolis of Lethbridge?"

"You're trying to tease me, Dr. Iverson." Whitaker smiled. "But I can tell you, with the ten million that I will make from this deal, you will have to do better than that to upset me."

"Ten million? You've sold Todd and me for a measly ten million?"

"Only you, Dr. Iverson. They really don't want your son."

I felt a cold shiver down my back.

Dad glanced at me and then looked down. "What are you planning?" he asked. He moved his hands under the table.

"Me? Oh, I'm planning on taking my money and retiring somewhere warm and sunny," Whitaker said.

I glanced down.

Dad had made claws with his fingers.

I nodded. Way ahead of you, Dad.

"There's a word for people like you, Whitaker."

"Rich?"

Slowly, very slowly, I began to undo my belt.

"Not the one I was thinking of, but we'll let it go."
Dad suddenly frowned. "So you are the one who killed Ms.
Scott."

"I never did!" Whitaker's smile disappeared and his
voice rose a bit. "I had nothing to do with her death!"

"Nothing?"

He took a deep breath, calming himself. "She was a
bit too opinionated," he said, finally. "They didn't like it."
He looked at us. "You don't know how ruthless these
people are. They will probably keep Todd alive, for the
time being. But only as leverage."

"Nice people you run with," Dad said.

"Rich people," Whitaker's smile was back. "And
that's all that matters!"

"It's never as simple as it seems," Dad said quietly.

"Beg your pardon?"

"Yes, I'm sure you will be."

"Enough talk. Get to your feet!"

Both dad and I slowly stood up.

The two men in black moved to the side of the room,
keeping their guns aimed at us, but allowing us passage to
the door.

Dad moved back to let me go first.

Bear! I thought and heard the satisfying rip of
material as my body responded to the command.

Whitaker spun around, just in time to get a face full
of claws. He screamed and dove behind the door.

The two soldiers were made of sterner stuff. One of
them pointed his gun and squeezed the trigger. The bullet

189

whined and ricocheted threateningly off walls and table, then finally stopped. Before the man could get a second shot off, I batted the rifle out of his hands and made a second swipe. At his chest.

Clutching his torn and bloodied uniform, he, too, found cover behind the door.

Then I turned to confront the second soldier.

But he was standing there with the most perfect expression of surprise on his face. As I watched, he lowered his gun, finally letting it fall. Then his legs buckled and he slowly sank toward the floor.

What on earth? It was then that I noticed the patch of red blooming against his dark shirt. The man had been shot.

By his partner's gun.

I watched, helplessly as his body settled onto the cold concrete. I turned to look at the other two, but they were out of sight behind the door.

Dad threw himself down beside the man and placed gentle fingers against his neck, then stripped open his shirt. There was a small hole directly over the man's heart. As they watched, a puddle of blood began forming under his body.

Dad sighed and shook his head. "There's nothing you can do, son." He got to his feet. "Let's get out of here before we're next!" He scooped up the two rifles and I followed him through the door.

Dad pulled the door shut and, breaking one gun open, wedged its 'L' shape between the door handle and jamb. Then he turned and looked at me.

"Which way?"

I shrugged massive shoulders and growled softly.

He looked back and forth. "We know what's behind us, but will we be able to access that exit?"

Well, someone must go out that way, I wanted to say.

There was a sudden thump on the door. Then a jerk on the knob. The door held. Fists began to bang on it. "Help! Someone help us!"

"They've killed Grimsby!" a second voice hollered.

Perfect.

Suddenly, we could hear the faint sound of excited voices. Dad turned his head. They were coming from further up the hall.

Decision made. We headed back to the circular room, praying we could find the exit.

In a hurry.

* * *

Dad craned his neck and circled the room again. "It's no use, son, I just can't see it," he sighed.

I stared upwards. Right there. I could almost see it. Right there. If only I were a fly on the wall.

Wait. In a heartbeat, I was circling the ceiling. Yes. Cracks there and there. But how to control them? Wait. More cracks. These started lower on the wall. More like a . . . door.

I followed the top one. A corner. Yes! A door!

I followed the crack to the ground. Then changed into myself and started to pull on the shreds of my clothes.

"What did you find, son?"

"There's a door here." I pointed with my chin as I pulled what was left of my shirt over my head.

Dad moved to the wall and began running his hands across it.

Suddenly, we both heard the sound of stone, sliding on stone. We spun around. The door was opening.

Dad raised the rifle and waited until the crack widened enough to see light. Then he sent a shot through it. We heard the bullet whine as it ricocheted off the walls.

191

The door snapped shut.

"Good shot, Dad! I didn't know you could shoot like that!"

"Gopher hunting," Dad said shortly. "But I'm afraid it won't hold them for long."

"Right." We both turned back to the wall.

"Where was that door?"

I moved closer and pointed. The cracks had been a lot easier to see as a fly.

Huh. That was a first.

"Ah! Right." Dad ran his fingers along the seam. "Yes. I see it now." He glanced at me. "Any idea how to open it?"

I shrugged. "I was lucky to figure out the seam."

"Hmmm." Dad ran his hand along the floor where it and the wall met. Something clicked. "Huh. I guess our good friend, Whitaker and my brother, Pete, both shop at the same hardware store."

"The same latch?"

"Exactly." Dad shoved on the wall. It slid open easily, revealing a long, dim hallway.

We both peered inside. "What do you think?" I said doubtfully.

"I'd say we have very few choices," Dad said. He glanced back at the other door. "And we know what's behind that door."

"Right." I charged down the new hall.

I could hear dad follow me into the tunnel, but then his footsteps stopped.

I skidded to a halt and turned to look at him. He was kneeling down beside the now-closed door and doing something to the latch. When he stood up, he was holding a long, thin piece of metal.

"What's that?"

He grinned. "The good thing about having the same equipment is knowing how it works." He nodded at the closed door. "Let's just say that it will take some time before they get that opened again."

"Brilliant!" I started up the hall once more. This time, I could hear Dad running behind me.

The hallway ended at a blank, block wall.

Dad knelt and fumbled along the floor. With a click, a section of the wall swung inward, disclosing a normal-looking basement.

"This must be the old man's house," Dad said. He darted across the room and started up a set of stairs.

"Who must be in on everything," I panted up behind him.

He grunted. Then, "A bear might just be of use, son."

"Done." Without pausing, I changed.

The door at the top of the stairs was locked, but I simply broke off the handle with one paw and shoved it open swinging out into a small hallway between a kitchen and laundry.

Directly ahead of us was the back door.

The man who had greeted us at the door such a short time before, was seated at the kitchen table, obviously preparing to enjoy his lunch. He stared at the two of us, his mouth a little 'O' of surprise.

"Don't bother to get up," Dad said, charging toward the door.

There was a gasp from the man and the clatter of something falling as I followed Dad into the open. I glanced over.

The elderly man had leaped from his chair and was backed against the kitchen wall, staring at me with wide and frightened eyes.

I simply nodded at him and followed my Dad.

The door opened into a tiny, but very tidy back yard. For just a moment, I could hear the sound of kids playing. Then something buzzed past my nose and buried itself in the wall of the house.

Then another.

What?

"Someone's shooting at us, Todd! Get back into the house!" Dad backed up, giving me a shove.

Ah. Bullets.

Great.

More of them zipped past me, striking the house and the door. From somewhere, I could hear someone screaming.

Dad pushed me inside and quickly pulled the door shut. "Get out of here, son!"

I moved away from the door, skidding to a stop mere inches from the staircase.

For a moment, I could still hear the thud of bullets as they continued spraying the house. Suddenly, they stopped.

Then I heard a different sound. Closer. A sort of . . . gurgle. I tilted my head. It seemed to be coming from the kitchen.

Turning, I caught my breath. The old man had collapsed onto the floor and was lying motionless.

I tried to shout, but all I could manage was a sort of growl. But Dad understood.

In a heartbeat, he was beside me, turning the man on his back and checking his breathing and pulse.

"He's in bad shape," he said. He pulled out his phone, dialled a number, and spoke briefly to the dispatcher. "Yeah, I don't know! Across the street north from the Catholic School. Just hurry!"

He began to work on the elderly man. Pumping his chest rhythmically.

Suddenly, we both heard a 'click'.

We looked up.

"Just so you don't get any more ideas," Whitaker said. A Whitaker with three long gouges across one cheek and blood dripping from his chin. He pulled the trigger.

Everything seemed to slow down. I heard the explosion of the gun, and tried desperately to get between the bullet and my dad. I could have saved my strength because it had been aimed at me.

I stared down stupidly at the hole it made.

Just below my ribcage.

I clapped a paw over it and looked into my dad's shocked eyes.

"Todd! Todd!" Dad said.

His voice faded.

Like the light.

Chapter Twenty-Two

I really didn't lose consciousness. Or if I did, it couldn't have been for very long. I opened my eyes slightly.

My head rested on the floor beside Dad, who was still crouched beside the old man and trying to continue his compressions with one hand. The fingers of Dad's other hand were pressed against my throat as he vainly tried to search for signs of life.

Whitaker was standing near the back door kitchen entrance, calm eyes on my Dad. A small stream of smoke curled from the barrel of his gun, which was still lifted toward us.

I winked at Dad. Or tried to.

He must have seen it. He gave a small sigh of relief and put both hands on the old man's chest once more. "Well, now we know just what you are capable of, Whitaker," he said, softly, grunting a little as he pumped.

"Yes, you do," Whitaker said. His gun clicked once more. "Don't make me use this again, Iverson," he said.

"You need me."

Whitaker sighed. "You're right," he said. Then he smiled. "But not all of you." The gun swung slowly along Dad's body. "You can still work from a wheelchair."

Dad stopped pumping and stared at the man.

"You are insane, Whitaker," he said bluntly.

Whitaker smiled again. "For wanting to be rich?"

"No, for what you're willing to do to be rich."

He shrugged. "I don't expect you to understand," he said. He pointed the gun again. "But I do expect you to cooperate."

Dad stopped what he was doing, then raised his hands and slowly got to his feet.

"That's much better," Whitaker said.

"What about this man?" Dad said. "What about Todd?"

"What about them?"

"Aren't you going to help them?"

"Dr. Iverson, you know better than to ask me that."

"But they'll die!"

"That's hardly my problem."

"Well, it could mean the difference between assault and murder."

Whitaker laughed. "You can't possibly think the law will catch up with me?!" he said incredulously. "I'll be rich! I can go anywhere!"

"Of course. How foolish of me," Dad said.

Suddenly, we could hear the sound of a siren.

Several sirens.

They grew louder.

"Ah. That would be the signal for us to disappear," Whitaker said.

Dad backed up a step. "Right," he said.

"This way, Iverson!"

Dad backed up another step. "I think we should go this way."

"Iverson!"

Dad dove out of sight through the opposite doorway.

Whitaker leapt across the old man and followed. But he had forgotten about me. Or maybe he thought I was in far worse shape than I was.

I threw out a paw.

Whitaker tripped, falling forward and hitting the floor with a heavy thud. The gun slid through the doorway and into the other room.

I pinned him where he had fallen.

He shrieked out something that was probably quite rude, but fortunately, unintelligible. I pressed more of my weight onto him and he soon shut up.

197

Ahh. That's better.

Dad reappeared through the door, holding the gun. "Everything okay, son?"

I looked up at him and nodded.

"Good. Are you all right?"

Dad knelt next to me and set the gun on the floor beside him. He moved his hands along my abdomen to the spot where the bullet had made its little entrance hole.

The wound had already sealed up and was looking decidedly . . . old.

"Any pain?"

I shook my head.

"Good." He looked down at Whitaker. "Can you hold him?"

I nodded.

He began working, once more, on the old man.

The sirens stopped just outside and we could hear the sound of many people shouting. Then someone started banging on what must have been the front door.

Dad looked suddenly harassed. "Come in!" he said. "I'm in the kitchen!"

More banging. More shouting. Finally, I heard the door burst open and footsteps pounding across the floor.

"In here!" Dad said again.

Several policemen, guns drawn, appeared in the doorway. And slid to a stop.

"Don't worry about the bear!" Dad said. "He's harmless. Just look after this guy. I'll look after the bear!"

"No! Help me! Help me!" Whitaker said.

I leaned on him a bit more.

He sputtered into silence.

"Ignore him!" Dad said. "Just come and help this man!"

The men trained their guns on me, but stepped forward just enough for two paramedics, dragging their equipment, to come into the room behind them.

"Hurry!"

The paramedics took positions beside the elderly man. "Doesn't look good," one of them said as he carefully checked vital signs.

Dad stood up. "When I found him five minutes ago, he was non-responsive," he said.

One of them glanced at him and nodded.

"I have been giving him chest compressions for . . . most of that time." Dad glanced at the man still pinned beneath me and frowned.

Another nod.

Dad reached down and picked up the gun by its barrel. Then he turned and handed it to one of the officers. The man took it gingerly and, checking it briefly, shoved it into his belt.

"I'm going to tell my bear to let this man, Whitaker, up," Dad said to the man. "But first I need you to know that Whitaker is responsible for the gunfire you were probably summoned over, and for kidnapping me and my son earlier."

"Pretty strong allegations, Mister . . .?"

"Iverson," Dad said. "Dr. Iverson. I can prove all I have to tell you," he went on. "And I'll hand my bear over to my brother, who is waiting out front, and accompany you to the station. But we do need to get this man locked up." He leaned closer. "I should probably tell you that he has connections with some pretty . . . powerful people."

The officers looked at each other and nodded. "Okay, Doc," one of them said. He pulled out his handcuffs. "Umm . . . tell your bear . . ."

While the officer was putting the cuffs on Whitaker, the paramedics rushed the old man out to their waiting

199

ambulance and raced away. Then the police officers lifted Whitaker to his feet.

The round little man glared at Dad. "We aren't finished yet," he said.

"I certainly hope not," Dad smiled. "I have a lot to say to you!"

Whitaker merely snorted.

The two officers lead him between them to the back door, then out to the miniscule back yard.

I could see more officers just across the back fence and several police cars parked on the strangely empty street.

Whitaker and his two escorts stopped at the gate. One of the officers bent down to push the latch.

Then, suddenly, something . . . popped. Whitaker gasped and fell forward, almost dragging his escorts with him.

More pops. Officers were shouting and scrambling for cover.

Someone was shooting!

Again.

Man. Did you ever have one of those days?

Dad and I dove behind the small shed beside the back door and peered around it.

Several things happened at once. A strange, black helicopter flew past. A helicopter that made . . . very little noise.

As we watched, a door slid shut in the side of it and the shooting stopped. Then, just before the copter slid out of our view, a window opened, disclosing a black-helmeted driver.

For just a moment, I felt eyes on me. I shivered.

Then the officers around us started returning fire. But, by this time, the helicopter was too far away for them to hope to do any damage. I could hear someone barking out orders nearby. Officers scrambled toward their cars and disappeared.

Then someone knelt down beside the crumpled body of Whitaker. "Well, he's gone," he said. "Call it in, Pops."

Another officer nodded and grabbed his radio.

"Hey, you!" someone said, "No one's allowed in here!"

"But my brother is in there!" Uncle Peter's voice.

"It's okay, officer!" Dad said. "He's with me."

"Who are you?"

"The man who can clear this whole thing up."

The officer stared at Dad for a moment, then nodded.

Uncle Peter came around the corner.

"Pete! I'm so happy to see you! I need you to take Todd. Then come to the station."

Uncle Peter nodded and reached for my arm. "C'mon, Todd. Have you had a rough day?"

I shuffled along beside him.

Police officers stepped back and watched us as we walked to the truck.

"Now what can I do to help?" I heard Dad's voice as I crawled inside.

* * *

Several hours later, Dad, Uncle Peter and I were still trying to tell our story to the Sergeant.

"So, what you are saying is that you have discovered something top secret and that Whitaker has been trying to sell your discovery to the highest bidder."

"In a nutshell," Dad said.

"Great. So what is this discovery?"

"I don't know if your clearance is that high," another voice said.

We all turned to see General Dune, standing in the doorway.

Strangely, I was happy to see the guy. Go figure.

The Sergeant looked up and sighed. "Another person who can 'clear this up'?"

The general smiled. "Actually, yes," he said. He moved forward and pulled out a chair. "So, where are we?"

Chapter Twenty-Three

Dad closed the door behind General Dune and his aide, then leaned against it weakly. "Well, at least that's over!"

"Over?" I stared at him. "It sounds like it's just starting!"

Dad grimaced, then turned and walked to the living room. There, he sank into a chair.

I sat down opposite him. "So what does it all mean?" I said.

He sighed. "Well, as nearly as we can tell, son, Whitaker pretty much conceived and carried out the plan by himself."

"Really?"

"Really. As soon as Ms. Scott told him about the Essence, he saw the great 'money making' possibilities and began contacting every military organization he could think of."

"Both good and bad?" I asked.

Dad nodded. "It didn't matter to him who they were, just how much they were willing to pay."

"Not what I'd call a sound business plan," Uncle Peter said as he walked into the room.

"Hey, Pete. Get that heifer taken care of?"

"She's all safe and comfortable in the barn, Bro," Uncle Peter said. "So, I saw the General's car go through the gate checkpoint. Are we finally rid of him?"

"Hardly," Dad said, his mouth twisting. "With the fences up all around the ranch and manned barricades and gates, I think we'll never be free of him."

Uncle Peter laughed. "Well, you're the one who invented the stuff!"

"Don't remind me!" Dad said. He sighed. "But at least it's finally in the hands of the Canadian and US militaries. Now they can look after it."

Uncle Peter nodded. "So did they discover if it was really Whitaker who killed Ms. Scott?"

"Well he said not, but can we believe anything he said?"

"Probably not," Uncle Peter said.

"I kinda feel sorry for her," I said.

Dad nodded. "As do we all."

"And General Doom had nothing to do with the attempts on Todd."

"Nothing. That was all Whitaker. Actually, I'm a little ashamed of my suspicions of Dune."

"Ashamed! When Dune kept you a prisoner?" Uncle Peter got up and walked over to the window.

"Well, he did tell us it was for our own protection," Dad said. He grimaced. "I guess we should have believed him."

"Yeah," I said. "Just because someone is talking to you through the bars of your cell, doesn't mean you can't believe what he is saying!"

Dad laughed. "It really wasn't that bad," he said, "except for not knowing where Todd was, or if he was all right."

"I was worried about you, too, Dad."

"Well, I don't think much of his way of doing things," Uncle Peter said.

"I don't, either," Dad agreed. "But I do believe he was desperate." He sighed. "He wants his boys in Iraq and other hotspots to come home alive. I guess if we have to accuse him of anything, it's of caring too much."

"Can you care too much?" Uncle Peter said.

Dad looked at me. "No," he said.

Uncle Peter nodded.

Just then, the doorbell rang.

"Anybody home?" JoJo's voice.

I jumped to my feet and met her coming around the corner.

"Todd!" She threw her arms around me. What is it about a hug that makes life look so much better? More particularly, JoJo's hugs.

I hugged back.

Dad cleared his throat. "Nice to see you, JoJo," he said. I could hear the smile in his voice.

We broke apart and turned to the two grinning men.

"Hi, Dr. I, Uncle Peter," JoJo said, her voice betraying no trace of embarrassment. She towed me over to the couch and sat down.

"So, what are we talking about?"

Have I mentioned that JoJo is my hero?

"We're just talking about things," Dad said, his grin widening. "Glad to have you join us."

"Good, 'cause you're stuck with me. Mom dropped me off at the gate, rather than endure the third degree herself." JoJo crossed her legs. "So if you want me to go, you'll have to take me."

Dad and Uncle Peter laughed.

"Fair enough," Dad said.

"So, what are we talking about?"

"Oh, how much we were mistaken in General Dune," I said.

JoJo made a face. "Yeah. I hate to admit it, but I was wrong, too. I thought he was behind everything. The scares. The kidnapping attempts."

"Yeah. Who would have figured him for the good guy?" I laughed.

"So did anyone ever find out who the poor old guy was?" JoJo said.

Dad made a face. "'Poor Old Guy' was just the new occupant of the house. Apparently, the only thing Whitaker told him was what to do if anyone asked for him or for his organization."

"Yeah." I grinned. "Go to the phone booth."

"I guess we can't accuse Whitaker of having no sense of humour," Dad said.

"And apparently, the old fellow didn't even know about the secret passage that connected his house with Whitaker's headquarters," I said.

"That would have been a shock," Dad said. "Imagine finding out that your house is actually an entrance to a top-secret installation."

"Yeah. If seeing Todd hadn't caused him so much grief, that probably would have done it."

"Poor fellow. I was sad when Todd told me he didn't make it."

"Yeah. That was pretty sad," I said.

She frowned. Then, "So do we know any more about the guys who shot Whitaker?"

Dad shrugged. "Could have been any one of a number of secret military organizations. "The only thing we do know is that it wasn't us or the U.S."

"Or anyone poor," Uncle Peter put in.

"Yeah. They were totally prepared to pay Whitaker 10 million," I said.

JoJo nodded. "Or at least said they would."

"And be convincing about it."

She nodded.

"From the police reports, the helicopter must have been sitting on a roof some distance away, waiting," Dad said. "The police hadn't even heard it approach."

"From what I read, it was one of the new 'stealth' copters. Not quite silent, but very nearly so," I said. "That would have been neat to see." I shivered suddenly. "Well, for more than a second as it blew past. And looked at me."

"When Whitaker came out in handcuffs and escorted by the police, his partners must have realized that their game had played out," Uncle Peter said. "Their first shot killed Whitaker instantly. The rest of the shots completely missed any of the policemen on the ground."

"Obviously intentional, in both cases," JoJo said.

"That kind of marksmanship isn't common. Or cheap," Dad said.

JoJo sat back in her chair. "Well, anyway, it's over."

"Well, this round, anyway." Dad grinned.

"I'd better get home and see what Bett has ready for supper," Uncle Peter said, getting to his feet.

"Speaking of supper, Jo, would you like some?"

She grinned at me. "You'll have to drive me off with a stick."

Epilogue

Dad and I were sitting across from each other in the living room a couple of days later.

"Well, I'm about all in," I said, starting to rise. "Time for bed."

"Just a moment, son," Dad said. "There's one more thing I need to talk to you about."

I settled back into my chair and looked at him expectantly.

He cleared his throat and rubbed a hand over his mouth.

"Spit it out, Dad," I said, grinning.

He looked at me and returned my grin. Weakly. "The thing is this," he said finally. "I haven't been entirely truthful with you, son."

I raised my eyebrows. "Really?"

"Really."

"How so?"

"Well, I knew that they were testing the Essence on someone," he said, "And I suspected that it was you."

"But you didn't know I was there."

He smiled, sheepishly. "I pretended to think that," he said. "Mostly, I was trying to convince myself. But the general let something slip a time or two and I . . . sort of put things together."

"So what's the problem with that?"

He took a deep breath. "Well, I know my reasoning might sound a bit . . . twisted, but it made sense to me at the time . . ." He paused.

"Dad. I'm right here. Tell me what it is."

He sighed again. "Well, I thought that if they were going to test the Essence on my son, and there was absolutely no way that I could stop them, then the next best thing I could do was . . . join him."

"Join . . .?"

"I also tested it on myself."

"You took every dose I did?"

"Almost. It got a bit more complicated when the Essence began lasting more than a few hours. Then I had to get creative. But, for most of the time I was in there, I experimented on myself before I sent it out to be tested on . . . you."

I stared at him. "You took all of the doses I did?"

"Most of them."

"But has it . . . affected . . ."

Suddenly I was staring at a cougar, sitting in my father's chair and, ludicrously, wearing my father's clothes.

My mouth dropped open.

The cougar slid gracefully from the chair and made a couple of circuits of the room, stopping finally beside me and bumping my hand with a hard, dry nose.

"Okay. Okay, I believe you!"

The cat moved back to Dad's chair and stepped up into it, settling itself once more.

"Okay, Dad. You can change back now."

But nothing happened.

"Dad?"

He shivered.

"Dad? You're starting to scare me. What's the matter? Change back! C'mon, it's easy. Just picture yourself! Your hands, body, fingers, toes!"

He shook violently and began to thrash around. Then tipped off the chair and fell with a thump onto the floor.

By now I was getting really alarmed.

"Dad? Just try! Just lay back and calm your mind and try!"

Dad flipped over and continued to flail his legs. His tail. He arched his back and let out a scream of agony.

"Dad!" I could feel tears on my cheeks. "Dad!"

209

Finally, he went still. For several moments, he lay there, breathing heavily. Then he sat up slowly and looked at me.

In his eyes I could see . . . was it pain? Fear?

"Dad?"

He shook his head. Something strangely like tears collected at the corners of the big cat eyes.

"Dad, can't you change?" My voice had gotten weak. It was hard to force the words out.

Another head shake.

"Dad!" I walked over to him and threw my arms around the heavily-muscled neck. I pressed my face into the soft, yellow hair.

For several minutes, the two of us sat there, curled together on the cold floor.

Finally, feeling chilled, I moved to a chair.

Dad sat beside me.

The two of us stared at each other.

"It's okay, Dad," I said, as calmly as I could. "We'll work it out."

The cat nodded, then shivered and sank back onto the floor.

I laid a hand on the soft hair.

"We'll work it out."

# # #

About the Author:

Photo Credit: David Handschuh

Born on a ranch in Southern Alberta and raised by a family of writers, Diane Stringam Tolley caught the bug early, publishing her first story at the age of 11. Trained in Journalism, she has written countless novels, articles, short stories, plays, songs and poems. Her Christmas books, Carving Angels and Kris Kringle's Magic have become perennial family favourites. Tolley and her Husband live in Northern Alberta and are the parents to six and grandparents to seventeen.

If you enjoyed <u>Essence: A Second Dose</u>,
You might also enjoy these books
By the same author
Available on Amazon:

The first volume in this series, Essence
Carving Angels
(Kris Kringles) Magic
Gnome for Christmas
SnowMan
Words
High Water

Find me at:
<u>https://twitter.com/StoryTolley</u>
https://www.facebook.com/diane.tolley1
https://ca.linkedin.com/in/diane-tolley-ab990626
https://www.smashwords.com/profile/view/greatw
eststoryteller
Blog: <u>http://dlt-lifeonthreranch.blogspot.ca</u>
Web Site: <u>http:// dianestringamtolley.com</u>

I'd love to hear from you!
<u>dtolley@shaw.ca</u>

Made in the USA
Columbia, SC
28 October 2017